WITHDRAWN THE
FLOODS
3

Home & Away

THE FLOODS

3

Home & Away

Colin Thompson

illustrations by the author

RANDOM HOUSE AUSTRALIA

This work is fictitious. Any resemblance to anyone living or dead is purely coincidental.

Random House Australia Pty Ltd
Level 3, 100 Pacific Highway, North Sydney NSW 2060
www.randomhouse.com.au

First published by Random House Australia 2006

Addresses for companies within the Random House Group can be found at www.randomhouse.com.au/offices

National Library of Australia
Cataloguing-in-Publication Entry

Thompson, Colin (Colin Edward).
    Home and Away.

    For primary school children.
    ISBN 978 1 74166 032 6.
    ISBN 1 74166 032 7.

    I. Title. (Series: Thompson, Colin (Colin Edward) The Floods; 3).

    A823.3

Design, illustrations and typesetting by Colin Thompson
Additional typesetting by Anna Warren, Warren Ventures
Printed and bound by Griffin Press

15 14 13 12

The Floods' Family Tree

MERLIN
Wizard

MORDONNA
Witch

Valla
Boy – 22

Satanella
Girl – 16

Merlinmary
Not sure – 15

Winchflat
Boy – 14

Morbid & Silent
Twin boys – 11

Betty
Girl – 10

This book is for my grandson Walter

who was born on 7 January 2006,
but is actually 287 years old.

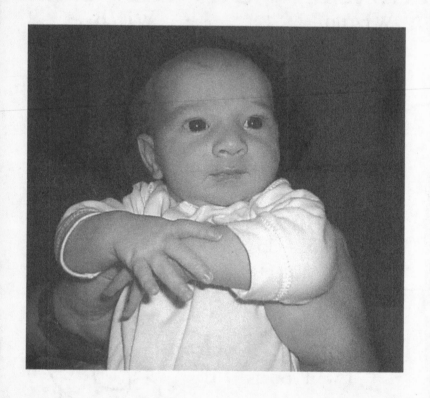

Prologue

If you haven't read the first two Floods books, you probably don't know that the Floods are a family of witches and wizards who live at numbers 11 and 13 Acacia Avenue – an ordinary street in an ordinary town, just the sort of place you or I might live.[1] (The little number you can see at the end of the previous sentence refers to a footnote at the bottom of this page. It does not mean there is something written on your foot.)

---

[1] *Actually, I don't live in an ordinary street in an ordinary town. I live near the Never Never River in a valley called The Promised Land. If you don't believe me, read about the area at http://www.bellingen.com.*

 is decorative; the page number 1 appears within it.

You can read all about Acacia Avenue and how the Floods came to own two houses and get rid of the neighbours from hell in the first Floods book, *Neighbours*.

Nerlin and Mordonna Flood have seven children. The eldest, Valla, has left school and is the manager of the local blood bank, a job he got by draining the blood out of the previous manager and all the other applicants who applied to replace him.

The next five Flood children go to a wonderful school for witches and wizards in Patagonia called Quicklime College. You can read all about this school – which makes Hogwarts look like a really boring TAFE – in the second Floods book, *Playschool*.

Betty, the youngest of the Floods, goes to an ordinary school a few streets away, and you'll be able to read about Sunnyview Primary School and Betty's nerdy new friend, Ffiona, in the next Floods book, *Survivor*.

Nerlin and Mordonna have not always lived

in Acacia Avenue. They both come from a land far, far away, a dark secretive country hidden in unmapped mountains and deep gloomy valleys between Transylvania and the endless pine forests of deepest Russia. You won't find it on a map, because any map-makers who have ventured into this land over the centuries have been turned into garden gnomes. This is not a place anyone ever visits for a holiday. In fact, it is the only country in the world without a tourist board.

Now read on . . .

1

The country where Mordonna and Nerlin were born is called Transylvania Waters. The witches, wizards, gremlins, zombies, corpses and other creatures of the night who live, or half-live, in Transylvania Waters are terrible snobs.[2] They are always showing off with things like turbo broomsticks and Versace magic wands covered in black sapphires. They are forever boasting how their skin is the whitest and their baby smells as if it has been dead longer than anyone else's. Nearly everyone in Transylvania Waters is like this, except the Dirt People.

---

[2] *The only humans there have been kidnapped from the outer world to be kept as pets by very rich witches.*

Although they are wizards too, the Dirt People spend their entire lives underground, cleaning the lavatories from below and burrowing up into coffins to nibble all the meat off the fresh corpses so their bones are sparkling white. The Dirt People are treated terribly. If an above-ground creature is feeling angry or mean – which they are most of the time, especially when they find their neighbour has skin that is two shades whiter than theirs – they pour boiling blood down the drain just to scald the Dirt People.

The Dirt People were once the noblest witches and wizards who ever lived. In fact, the most famous wizard of all, Merlin, was himself one of the Dirt People. Exactly how they were reduced to living such terrible, oppressed lives is a long and complicated story involving international intrigue, huge amounts of gold, extremely white skin, badly fitting tights and a beige cockerel called Norman, a story that may well be revealed at a later date.

Nerlin Flood was one of the Dirt People and a direct descendant of Merlin, but he knew little of

his glorious ancestry. Until he was twelve, he never even saw the light of day, unless it was the weak glow reflected down the lavatory bowls above him. There were no teachers or school for the children of the Dirt People, who huddled together in damp tunnels and caves. Their only education was in the art of drain navigation and lavatory cleaning, so that when they began work at the age of twelve and someone shouted, 'Grease and gristle blockage at 17 Goitre Street!' they would know where to go and what hat to wear.

This life had turned the Dirt People into a downtrodden, flushed-over race of beings who were too defeated to even feel depressed. They may have once ruled the world and had great magic at their fingertips, but an evil spell had been cast over them to make them forget. Even if it dawned on someone that there could possibly be a better life somewhere else, there was no escape. The manhole covers were bolted down and the outlets barred with heavy steel gratings.

Sometimes the spirit of Nerlin's ancestor, the

legendary Merlin, spoke to Nerlin while he was asleep, but all Nerlin could hear was a faint crackling whisper and the occasional word like 'Excalibur' and 'Belgium'. It was enough to make him realise there might be something else to life, somewhere else to live – somewhere that didn't grow mould that tried to eat you, maybe a place where it was bright enough to not keep banging into things.

'Now, now, son,' said his father. 'Thoughts like that only lead to unhappiness.'

'I thought that was where we lived already,' said Nerlin.

'Just accept life as it is, or you'll end up like Uncle Knute.'

No one would ever tell him how Uncle Knute had ended up, but Nerlin imagined it was not very nice as all that remained of his uncle was a pincushion made of his left buttock.

So the years passed and Nerlin tried to stop thinking. He immersed himself in his work as a lavatory-from-beneath cleaner, which was not pleasant. Sometimes in the evenings he would go

and sit by the big grating where all the drains flowed out over the sheer drop into Lake Tarnish. There he could dream to his heart's content, at least for a few precious minutes, until the toxic chemicals that floated softly in the fumes made large pieces of his skin start falling off. Nerlin would then crawl away to his bed of mouldy paper and dream of what might lie beyond the yellow fumes. He knew so little that all he could imagine was more fumes, maybe in a different colour.

And then, one wonderful day, when Nerlin was eighteen years old, everything changed. Something unheard-of happened, something so magical that it must have been fate.

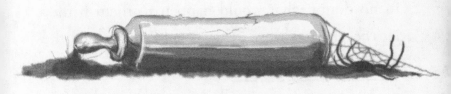

Mordonna was also eighteen, and was ravishingly beautiful. She was the most beautiful girl in the whole

of Transylvania Waters, and to make it even more unfair on all the other girls in the country, she was also the heir to the throne, the eldest daughter of King Nombre-Sept-À-Quatorze.[3] To make it triply unfair, she was staggeringly intelligent, a brilliant cook and had very, very, very white skin and extremely well-fitting tights.

But Mordonna was a prisoner of her own wonderfulness, for this poor creature had spent her entire life in the castle. The tall walls that surrounded the castle gardens were a jail that she was never allowed to leave. Since no one would ever be good enough to be allowed to marry Mordonna, the King had all the gates locked except one, and that was guarded by two giant Cyclops, who were in no doubt what would happen to them if they let the princess leave. They would be granted the King's favourite gift, the gift he liked to give to

[3] The King's full title is eighteen pages long and includes words from fifteen different languages. This makes ceremonial occasions in Transylvania Waters long, dreary affairs because it can take hours just to read his name out. In this book we will call him King Quatorze for short.

his enemies. They would go water-skiing on Lake Tarnish.[4]

Throughout her childhood, Mordonna had spent many hours crouched at the foot of the castle wall, listening to the world outside. She could hear

---

[4] *The longest distance anyone has ever water-skied on Lake Tarnish is fifteen metres. The record holder wore a very thick rubber suit and skied twelve of the metres on land before entering the water. On moonlit nights the surface of the lake is lit with an eerie glow. It is the radioactive light from the bones of past water-skiers.*

the hustle and bustle of the town, the talking and shouting and laughing. She could taste the air with its exciting smells as the common people lived their strange and fascinating lives. Even the birds that sometimes flew over the wall seemed brighter and happier than those that lived around the castle. Her heart overflowed with loneliness and misery.

'I wish I could just be an ordinary person like everyone else,' she would say to any of the servants who would listen.

'Yeah right,' they would reply, totally not believing a word of it.

'Who does she think she is?' they would say to each other later. 'She has everything times ten that anyone could dream of and all she can do is moan about it.'

Mordonna's only happiness was her garden, where she grew every poisonous plant known to man, from deadly nightshade to the Destroying Angel mushroom.[5] She fed them to her sister, Howler.

Howler was everything Mordonna was not: stupid, ugly, the proud possessor of a spectacular lump, with three eyes, several green teeth and a map of Belgium tattooed on her left leg. Howler also wore the baggiest tights in the whole of Transylvania Waters, and in the baggiest bit round the ankles she kept her pet leech, Queasymodo, and several families of slugs in case she felt a bit peckish between meals. It was impossible to tell if she was older or younger than Mordonna – especially as she spent most of her life in a cellar full of warty

---

[5] *There really is a mushroom called the Destroying Angel and it is SERIOUSLY poisonous.*

toads where, at least, no one thought she was ugly. In fact, it was hard to imagine the two sisters were even related apart from the beautiful eyelashes they both shared, though Mordonna's only grew on her eyelids.

'Couldn't you do some magic and make me beautiful like you?' Howler begged Mordonna.

'I don't think there's a spell that would be powerful enough,' Mordonna replied.

She felt sorry for Howler and did try. She experimented on one of the warty toads, but it ended up worse rather than better. The sight of her creation – a 25-kilogram purple warty toad that croaked in Belgian and wore tights that were so baggy it couldn't hop more that a few centimetres without tangling itself up in a knot – made Mordonna too scared to have another go.

'At least you have your freedom,' she said to Howler. This is because the King, realising Howler's chances of finding true or even false love were almost nil, did not keep her confined to the castle grounds. In fact, he encouraged her to go out

as often as possible in the hope that someone or something would come along and take her off his hands. She usually ended up at the sewerage works, where she felt most at home.

While he kept Mordonna a prisoner, King Quatorze sent secret agents around the world to find a prince worthy of Mordonna's hand.

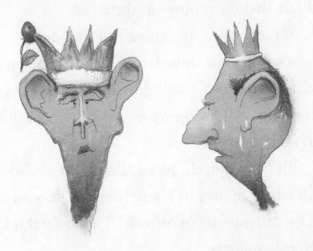

'He must be incredibly handsome, incredibly intelligent and incredibly rich – and of course he has to be a prince,' said the King. 'That is all I ask. Go and find me a Prince Charming.'

His agents searched high and low.

'All right then,' said the King as he tore up the last of the photos. 'He must look fairly human, be not too stupid and seriously incredibly rich.'

The King's agents had another look.

'Well,' the King sighed as he tore up the new batch of photos, 'just find someone staggeringly rich and still breathing and preferably with a chin and ears that don't move in the wind.'

Which, of course, ruled England out.

'Daddy,' said Mordonna, as she tore up the final four photos, 'I will go water-skiing on Lake Tarnish in a blotting-paper bikini before I will marry any of them.'

'But, my angel,' pleaded the King, who had spent all the money in Transylvania Waters on cake and garden gnomes of himself, 'I am only thinking of your happiness.'

'And what makes you think my happiness is linked to your wallet?' snapped Mordonna.

'I am the King,' roared the King. 'That means everyone has do what I tell them, including you.'

Mordonna went to her mother, Queen

Scratchrot, to see if she could call the King off, but all the Queen could say was, 'I've been telling him he's off for years, dear. But you know what he's like when he gets a bee in his bonnet.'

'Then I shall have to escape,' said Mordonna.

'Yes, of course you shall, my dear,' said her mother, and turned back to her cobweb weaving.

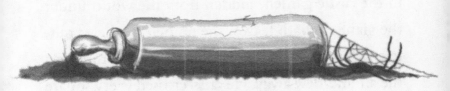

On the day Mordonna had been born, a large vulture had flown in through the window and sat at the foot of the bed. Many people said that this was a fantastic omen that meant something really significant, but no one was sure what. The King's personal soothsayer, Bloodlyss, muttered about signs of great portent and future massive importance, but wasn't prepared to commit herself in case she was wrong. The King made her go water-skiing.

Mordonna's first word had not been 'Mama' or

'Papa' but 'Leach', which had become the vulture's name.[6] Leach followed Mordonna everywhere and over the years child and bird developed a strange telepathic relationship that could only exist between a staggeringly beautiful princess and a really ugly bird with a bald neck.

Now, as Mordonna sat in her special place in the castle garden, hidden from the world under the giant rhubarb leaves, she poured her heart out, telepathically, to the wise old bird. Leach rose into the air and flew away. He criss-crossed every square metre of the palace ground and, as afternoon finally gave way to evening, he returned to his beloved mistress.

'Follow me,' he telepathed.[7]

He led Mordonna to a scrubby patch of ground behind one of the sheds and began to peck

---

[6] *What Mordonna had been trying to say was 'Leak', which was what her nappy had been doing, but as she was looking at the bird when she said it, everyone had assumed that she had been trying to talk to it.*

[7] *Yes, yes, I know it's not a proper word, but I like it and you know what it means.*

at the earth with his beak. He grabbed the few lonely flowers in his claw and ripped them out of the ground.

'Come on,' he telepathed. 'Dig.'

'But I'll get my hands dirty,' Mordonna telepathed back.

'Do you want to get out of here or not?'

'What? You mean...? Wow,' Mordonna whispered. She began to dig too and, as she pulled on a particularly large, revoltingly orange marigold, the ground collapsed beneath her and she fell into a deep dark hole.

At the bottom of the deep dark hole was a drain that young Nerlin was cleaning, and by an amazing but obviously pre-destined coincidence, Mordonna landed right on top of him.

'What the...?' Nerlin exclaimed, face-down in the sludge.

'Who the...?' cried Mordonna, jumping up.

She opened her mouth to scream, but Nerlin had lifted himself out of the sludge and was wiping his face on his sleeve, and something in the young

man's eyes made her stop. A sparkle there went straight into a soft bit of Mordonna's brain that, until this very moment, had been fast asleep. She knew she should be screaming because a filthy stinking drain was not a place a princess should be, but the light in Nerlin's eyes held her entranced.

She tried to speak, but no words would come out of her mouth, which surprised her because she knew thousands of them.

'Who … err, err?' she finally managed to say.

Nerlin was also speechless. There was a sparkle in Mordonna's eyes, too. She was the most incredibly beautiful creature Nerlin had ever seen, so beautiful that he thought she could not be a real

person, but an angel that had fallen from heaven. Which she was, sort of, except angels don't usually fall on top of you and fill your nose up with slime.

After what seemed like an hour of staring at each other, they calmed down enough to talk.

'Umm,' said Nerlin.

'Yes,' Mordonna added.

'Sorry,' Nerlin continued.

'Yes, quite,' said Mordonna, then, 'What for?'

'Being underneath you.'

'Oh,' said Mordonna.

Then she thought for a bit and did something she had never ever done one single time in her whole life up until that point. She apologised.

'Sorry for falling on top of you,' she said. 'Would you like me to move?'

'Well, my legs have gone numb, but umm…' Nerlin began, but he was too shy to tell her he didn't want her to move.

'OK,' said Mordonna. Neither of them moved.

After what seemed like another hour passed and Nerlin's legs had turned a scary shade of blue

with green bits, they managed to move and sat facing each other, both glad they had enough muck on their faces to hide their blushes.

Mordonna had led a very sheltered life. Her only teacher had been forbidden to talk to her because she was a commoner and Mordonna was a very important princess. So although it had been very peaceful in the classroom, apart from Howler eating school books in a box in the corner, Mordonna had only learnt the few things the teacher had written on the blackboard. She knew the principal towns and exports of Belgium, how to tie her shoelaces and fifteen exciting things to cook in French using the limbs or insides of helpless amphibians. The millions of things she had never even heard of included the Dirt People, and when Nerlin told her about them she was horrified.

'That's terrible,' she said. 'Making you live down here in the dark like rats. Nice smell, though, isn't it?'

'I don't know,' said Nerlin. 'I've never smelled anything else.'

'Here, try this,' Mordonna said. She held her armpit close to Nerlin's face. He closed his eyes and took a deep sniff. He couldn't speak. His doubts were swept away. He knew he was deeply, incredibly, head-over-knees, in love.

'Can I smell yours?' said Mordonna, cuddling up to him.

She closed her eyes and buried her nose in Nerlin's muddy armpit. She was in love too. All the years of loneliness were swept away. She had met her destiny.

Their happy underarm-sniffing was interrupted by a roar from above. It was King Quatorze. The roar basically said that Nerlin was more worthless than a festering speck of snot embedded in a mouldy blob of slug slime, and that because he had touched the King's daughter, the King was going to turn him into a septic-truffle, have him eaten by a vampire frog and then kill him before teaching him to water-ski.

'But I love him, Father,' cried Mordonna.

The King went very, very red, opened his

mouth, closed it again, went redder than the reddest thing in the universe, and exploded. Bits of him landed on Nerlin and Mordonna. The lovers leapt to their feet and ran down the drain into the darkness.

'They'll come after me,' said Mordonna. 'My father will never rest until he catches us.'

'But ... I thought he just exploded,' said Nerlin.

'Oh, he does that all the time,' Mordonna said.

2

The Drains

'Fifty million gold sovereigns, three-point-seven hundredths of my Kingdom and the hand of my other daughter, Howler, in marriage to the person who brings back my precious daughter and kills the vile traitor who has kidnapped her!' roared the King.

'There's only me out here, dear,' said Queen Scratchrot through the door. 'Besides,' she added, 'who would want to marry poor Howler?'

King Quatorze dropped six sticks of dynamite and a hand grenade into the toilet, in the hope that Nerlin would be in the drain below, and pulled the chain.

'That'll teach him,' he said, coming out of the batroom, which is like a bathroom only with bats hanging above your head watching you.[8]

I think you need to calm down a bit, dear,' said the Queen. 'If this person *has* actually kidnapped Mordonna, which I doubt, and he *is* actually in the drains where your dynamite comes out, and it *does* actually kill him, then it will probably kill her too.'

The King looked disgruntled. 'Right ... well, I'll ... umm, I'll get the Chancellor to make a proclamation.'

'Now, Nombre, you don't actually have fifty million gold sovereigns, do you?' said the Queen.

'Well, no, not as such,' said the King. 'I do have some nice fruit cake and lots of spare garden gnomes.'

'You don't even have five gold sovereigns, do you?'

---

[8] *If you want to be a writer, here is a tip. Keep your eyes and brain open. I invented the batroom when I typed bathroom with a letter missing by mistake.*

'Err, umm, well … no,' the King admitted. 'But the rescuer will be so entranced by Howler they might not notice.'

'I think *entranced* is probably not the right word, is it, dear?' said the Queen. 'I think the word is more like *eaten*.'

'Probably,' said the King. 'They certainly won't notice then, will they? And anyway, when our beautiful Mordonna is married to Prince Nochyn of Battenberg we will have a *hundred* million gold sovereigns.'

'But she doesn't love him,' said the Queen. 'She will never marry him.'

'Love? Love? What's not to love about a hundred million gold coins?'

When the King had calmed down some more, Queen Scratchrot sent him off to find the Chancellor, then she summoned her faithful equery, Vessel.[9]

'My lady,' said Vessel, kneeling before her.

---

[9] *An equery is an equerry who asks a lot of questions.*

Beneath the hood of his cloak, Vessel's face appeared to be no more than two small piercing eyes set in black emptiness. In his right hand he carried his staff: a dead tree with a bird's nest at the top. In the nest of broken dusty twigs lived Vessel's crow assistant, Parsnip. Parsnip spoke a strange pigeon English, which everyone apart from pigeons found very confusing.

Vessel worshipped Queen Scratchrot. Every second of every minute of every hour of every day, he held her image close to his heart on a platinum chain around his neck. To make sure there was never an instant when he wasn't thinking of her, the chain was woven with sharp spines that constantly pricked

his skin and drew tiny drops of blood. In his private quarters up in one of the castle's many towers he had over thirty-two boxes of the Queen's toenail clippings, three sacks of her hair, and a jar of small flaky bits of unspecified origin. The Queen herself pretended to be completely unaware of Vessel's adoration. Or, more accurately, she pretended to pretend to be unaware, because she was actually in love with Vessel and not the King, because Vessel was everything the King was not – taller than her, intelligent and a sensitive seeker of wisdom. Also, his tights fitted really well and had almost no runs in them.

'My good and faithful servant,' said the Queen, 'I want you to go down into the drains and make contact with the Dirt People. Find out who this man is that Mordonna has fallen in love with and tell her that, if she really does love him, I will do all I can to help them.'

'My lady, you are, as ever, kind, wonderful and overflowing with bounteous wisdom.'

'I hardly need add,' the Queen added, 'that

this must be done with the utmost secrecy. As you know, my husband has spies everywhere.'

'You can count on me, your highness,' said Vessel, licking the Queen's shoes. Then, feeling dizzy, he added, 'Oh my great queen, pray tell me what is that wonderful flavour in your shoe polish?'

'Patagonian Bat Guano.'

'Greater-Spotted Patagonian Bat or Hawk-mouth Patagonian Bat, my queen?'

'Greater-Spotted,' the Queen replied. She felt herself blush and turned her face away before whispering, 'Your favourite.'

'I will find your daughter,' said Vessel, getting up slowly so as not to pass out. 'You can count on me.'

'I know I can. I don't know how I would manage without you,' said the Queen. 'Here, have some of my bellybutton fluff.'

Vessel nearly fainted with pure delight. He dropped his tree, sending Parsnip flapping up onto the curtains in a flurry of pigeon swear

words. Leaving the bird behind, Vessel crawled backwards out of the room and slipped silently down the stone stairs into the cellars. From there, he made his way down three more levels into the deepest dungeons where the King kept all the people who wouldn't give him any more money – the members of parliament, prime ministers and bank managers.

At the end of the darkest, dampest tunnel there was a small door that looked as if it hadn't been opened for a hundred years. It looked like this because it hadn't been opened for a hundred years. Vessel had entered the castle through this very door one hundred and one years earlier as a young man. No

one, not even the Queen, knew that Vessel had been born one of the Dirt People. He had kept his head down and blended into castle life, starting as an apprentice cabbage leaf polisher and working his way up until he was now one of the most powerful people in the land. The King hated him because the Queen liked Vessel better than she liked him. And even though it would have been easy to have him destroyed, the King knew that if he did, the Queen would destroy *him*.

The door was thick with a century's cobwebs. Yet when Vessel took a rusty key from his pocket and inserted it in the lock, it turned with no effort at all. It was as if someone had been oiling it.

There was something behind the door. When Vessel pushed it open, the something fell over with a feeble cry.

'Is that you, Vessel?' said an ancient spindly voice from under a broken chair.

'Mother?' said Vessel.

'Yes. Come here, my child, that I may feel your face. My eyes left me many years ago as I sat here

waiting for your return,' said the old lady, wiping her oily hands on her dress.

'You mean … every day, for a hundred years?'

'Yes, I knew you'd come.'

Vessel waited for the old lady to move, but she didn't.

'Oh dear,' she said at last. 'I've been sitting here for so long I seem to have forgotten how to move.'

Vessel picked up his mother and carried her down the narrow drain into the sewers. She was so frail that Vessel imagined he was holding a bundle of sticks.

'See, everybody,' the old lady kept calling out, 'I told you he'd come back.' But there was no one there.

The sewer joined others and finally led into the Great Sewer of Quagmire. Here and there people appeared wearing the traditional lavatory cleaner's Wide Hat and carrying their long brushes. The heady smell of rotting food and other drainy substances filled Vessel's head with long-forgotten memories. A little voice inside his head kept telling him that he had come home, but his heart told him that his home now was up above with his beloved queen.

They passed under the town that surrounded the castle and out past its suburbs towards the end of the Great Sewer, where it poured its untreated effluent from a hole in a cliff high above Lake Tarnish. The mouth of the drain was blocked off with a heavy cast-iron grating put there by the King's ancestors to keep the Dirt People from escaping. The secret door to the castle that Vessel had gone through was the only way in or out of

the entire drainage system.[10] Apart from occasional gas explosions in the drains and the faint glow that sometimes shone down from the lavatories, the grating was the only source of light in the whole sewer system. It was in the side tunnels near this grating that the Dirt People had made their homes.

Vessel carried his mother through the honeycomb of narrow tunnels with an inherited skill that all Dirt People had from birth, only hitting her head on the low roof seventeen times. Even though it was a full century since he had gone to the world above, Vessel needed no guidance to his old family home. The route would be forever etched into his memory.

'Where the hell have you been, Mother?' said Vessel's father as they entered. 'It's a new century.'

You would think that Vessel's father would be over the moon with excitement to be reunited with

---

[10] *Except, of course, for the hole that Mordonna had fallen down, though the King had since filled that in with ten tonnes of concrete.*

his only son after a hundred years, but he had lived in the drains all his life and he had never seen or even heard of the moon. Besides, being a hundred and fifty or so, he had reached the age where all he wanted to do was sit and stare at the wall and watch the slime and algae grow.[11]

'Who are you?' said Vessel's dad.

'Your son,' Vessel replied. 'Are those new shoes you're wearing?'

After his dinner had gone down, come back up and gone down again, Vessel asked around the tunnels to find the princess. At first people were suspicious of him, but they knew that once a Dirt Person, always a Dirt Person, and so they took him to where Nerlin and Mordonna were hiding.

'Your royal highness, Princess Mordonna, I have been sent to speak with you by your mother, the great and glorious and wonderful and adorable Queen Scratchrot,' he said.

'Old man, I know you are a good and faithful

---

[11] *Or, as it was known in the drains, dinner.*

servant, but you must tell my mother that we are in love and I shall never return,' said Mordonna.

'You are in love?' Vessel asked. 'Both of you?'

'Yes.'

'With each other?'

'Yes,' said Mordonna. 'We are engaged to be married. Look.'

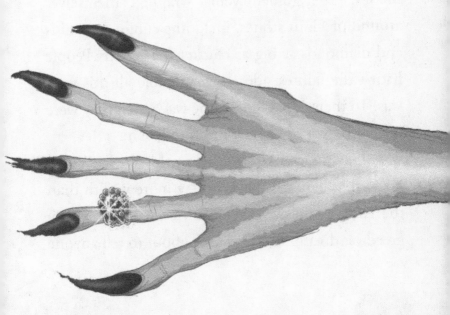

She held out her left hand and on her finger was an enchanted ring, woven from threads of the

finest gold. In its centre was a massive emerald surrounded by thirteen perfect diamonds.

What neither the King nor anyone else in the world above knew was that the drains led off into tunnels with walls covered in veins of the purest gold, not just little nuggets and specks, but veins as thick as your finger than ran for hundreds of metres. The golden veins wrapped themselves around precious stones, including rubies, emeralds and diamonds as big as chickens. The Dirt People hadn't the faintest idea how valuable all this stuff was. To them it just got in the way when they were trying to excavate a new room to live in.

Having moved to the world above, Vessel knew that beneath the town lay more wealth than the King could ever dream of, even in his totally greediest dream. But he wasn't about to tell anyone

about it, not even his beloved queen. Mordonna was overwhelmed when she saw the treasure, but she too decided she would never tell her father. Nevertheless, she did fill her pockets with enough diamonds to keep them for the rest of their lives.

'So, Vessel, you can tell my mother to tell my father I shall never return to the castle until he gives our love his blessing.'

'Well, your wonderful mother, my divine Queen, sends you *her* blessing and says she will do all she can to help you,' said Vessel. 'But I fear, young mistress, that nowhere in Transylvania Waters will be safe for you to hide. Your father will never accept this liaison. He planned to sell you in marriage to Prince Nochyn of Battenberg for one hundred million gold sovereigns, and he has already spent the ten per cent deposit.'

'I know,' said Mordonna. 'He'd sell my mother and my sister and me for nineteen pieces of silver. I've heard he even sold his aunt for a second-hand lawnmower. We will have to leave Transylvania Waters.'

'But there is no way out of the tunnels,' said Nerlin despondently. 'We are doomed to a life of darkness and slime.'

'Actually, there is a way out,' said Vessel. 'How do you think I got down here?'

'I imagined that as you are such a devoted servant to my mother you had allowed her to flush you down a lavatory,' said Mordonna.

'No, no, young mistress,' said Vessel, and told them about the secret door. 'My grandfather showed it to me and that was how I left the drains in the first place.'

'Can you take us to my mother?' said Mordonna. 'If anyone will know what to do, it will be her.'

'Yes, my lady. As soon as the world is asleep, we will go to the Queen.'

Queen Scratchrot may have been short-sighted, but she knew a hunk when she saw one, and as soon as she laid eye[12] on Nerlin she was captivated.

'I can see why you fell for him,' she said to her daughter. 'He's absolutely gorgeous.'

'Oh, mother,' Mordonna cried, 'what can we do? What is to become of us?'

'You must leave Transylvania Waters,' said the Queen. 'And I shall leave with you.'

'You would give up everything you have here, your majesty?' said Nerlin.

'I think you can call me Mummy now,' the Queen giggled. She tried to flutter her eyelids at Nerlin, but one of them fluttered out of the window and got attacked by a butterfly. 'Anyway, what's to give up? I've spent most of my life married to a red-faced, brainless, chinless tyrant. I know, I know, that's the role of every queen … but it's time for a change.'

'You would leave Transylvania Waters and

---

[12] *Only one, because her right eye always faced magnetic north.*

those who love you?' Vessel sobbed, unable to hide his true feelings.

The Queen patted her equery on the arm and whispered in his ear, 'Only if you will go with me, my dear.'

You would think that being married to a King would have its good points, such as wealth and status, but being the wife of King Quatorze had so many bad points – too many to list here – that Queen Scratchrot was very lonely. For years and years she had tried not to fall in love with her faithful equery, but his elegant dead-body-like good looks and sweet rotting-flesh smell made him irresistible. Now that her own daughter had found true love, the Queen decided she would deny her heart no more.

Vessel fainted and dropped his tree again, which made Parsnip *really* cross as he had only just settled back into his nest.

'Snip-Snip got head saw,' he squawked. 'Need go wet.'

'What's that bird talking about?' said

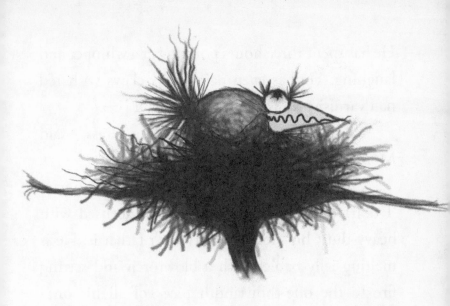

the Queen. 'Need go wet? Does he want to go to the toilet?'

'No. Need go wet,' Parsnip repeated. 'Snip-Snip got head saw, need go wetinary surgeon.'

The Queen threw a bucket of ice-cold water over Vessel, and when he had regained consciousness they all went down into the drains, where they would be safe from the King and his spies.

'There is no time to lose,' said the Queen when they were safely back in Nerlin's home in the sewers. 'You must marry this very night. The King is more wild with rage than I have ever seen him.

He has spent three hours pointing at a whippet and laughing. He has even painted its claws with red nail varnish and is calling it Margaret.'

'But I don't have a wedding dress,' said Mordonna.

'There's no time for that,' said the Queen. 'I don't think you realise just how incensed with heavy-duty, big-time furiosity your father is. He is melting jelly-babies with a blowtorch and setting fire to the one-thousandth piece of all his one-thousand piece jigsaw puzzles.'

'There's no such word as furiosity,' said Mordonna.

'There is now. I am the Queen so I'm allowed to invent words. Nerlin, my dear boy, go and fetch a marriage celebrant. There's no time to lose.'

'My father can perform the ceremony,' said Nerlin.

'Really?' said the Queen.

'Yes,' said Nerlin's father. 'I have passed through the sacred fire of the Curry Sewer. This gives me powers of authority. I have fought and

beaten the Great Greasetrap Alligator. This gives me the status of commander. I have swum through the Slough of Diced Carrots and emerged unscathed. This gives me –'

'Yes, yes, fine,' snapped the Queen.

'And I have my own pen,' Nerlin's father concluded.

'OK, OK, get on with it,' said the Queen. 'We have to go.'

'Dearly beloved,' Nerlin's father began, 'we are gathered –'

'Faster!' snapped the Queen.

'Do you, Mordonna, Princess of Transylvania Waters, take –'

'Of course she does, and so does he! Get on with it!'

'OK, I now pronounce you man and wife. You may kiss the bridge.'

'Don't you mean kiss the bride?' said the Queen.

'Not until he's kissed the brown bridge over the Great Sewer of Quagmire,' said Nerlin's father.

'It completes the ceremony. We all have to do it when we get married, and I can tell you it tastes dreadful.'

The wedding party walked to the bridge. Nerlin closed his eyes, took a deep breath and kissed the disgusting bridge. When it kissed him back he almost fainted.

'I must take you back to the castle, my lady,' said Vessel to the Queen, 'before the King notices you are missing.'

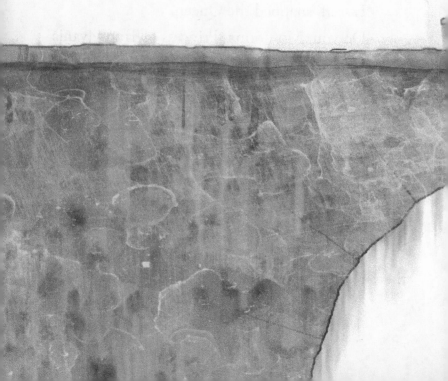

'Notices I'm missing?' laughed the Queen. 'You must be joking. If I vanished altogether he probably wouldn't notice for six months until it was time for his next bath and he wanted me to scrub his back.'[13]

---

[13] *The King's back was as smooth and lovely as a half-rotted hippopotamus's armpit. While the King hung on to the bath taps and shut his eyes, the Queen scrubbed him down with an angry porcupine on a very long stick. It was something she wouldn't miss when she ran away.*

The Dark Forest

'Have you located my daughter and the sewer rat who kidnapped her?' roared the King.

'I have, sire,' the Chancellor lied.

Baines LeClaude had been Chancellor for forty years. He had learnt after two minutes in the job to tell the King whatever he wanted to hear, whether it was true or not. When the information wasn't true the Chancellor would find someone lower down the line to blame. This way the Chancellor had managed to keep his head joined onto his body while many of his servants hadn't.

'You know exactly where they are then?' said the King.

'I do, sire.'

'And you have a plan to bring my beloved daughter safely back to me and kill her abductor in a really horrible, slow, painful and loud way?'

'It is in hand, sire,' the Chancellor lied, seeing a horrible brick wall appear inside his head with no door in it to escape through.

'You have two hours,' said the King. 'Oh, and one more thing before you go.'

'Yes, oh exalted one?' grovelled the Chancellor as he backed away towards the door.

'You have just told me your fifteen thousand, seven hundred and fifty-third lie since you became Chancellor. Each time you have managed to squirm out of blame by sacrificing some poor innocent idiot. Now, whilst I always enjoy beheading innocent idiots, I'm really looking forward to seeing how you get out of this one.'

'But sire …' the Chancellor began.

'Shut up,' said the King. 'It's simple. Princess Mordonna standing here before me safe and sound in two hours equals Chancellor's body and head

in the same room together. Princess Mordonna not standing here in two hours equals Chancellor's body and Chancellor's head in buckets on their way to the Export Burger Factory.'

'I ... I ... I ...'

'That's all. Now off you go and fetch my darling little Princess,' said the King. 'And on your way out, send in my secretary. We need to arrange for Prince Nochyn to come so we can marry them off before she tries anything like this again.'

'I'm a dead man,' the Chancellor cried to his wife.

'If I had a gold sovereign for every time I've heard you say that,' said his wife, 'I'd be really rich.'

'This time it's true,' the Chancellor said. He told his wife about Mordonna.

'In that case, yes, you're absolutely right,' said his wife. 'You *are* a dead man. Oh well, I suppose I'd better start looking for a new husband. Where's the evening paper?'

'*What!*' the Chancellor cried. 'Is that all you can say?'

'No, of course not,' said his wife. 'Before you go, don't forget to give me your bank books and the combination to your safe.'

The Chancellor fell on the ground and curled up into a little ball. His wife, who had been vacuuming the floor when he had come home with his news, was not completely heartless and decided to clean around him rather than make him move. His children were not so considerate and complained that they couldn't see the TV properly with him lying there.

'I suppose I might just as well kill myself now then,' sobbed the Chancellor.

'Yeuww, Dad, gross!' said his eldest daughter.

'Yes, too much information, Dad,' said the middle sister.

'Yeah, Dad, show some consideration. We've had a hard day at school,' said the youngest daughter. 'Go out and do it in the garden.'

RATBIX
90% TASTE FREE

EXPORT BURGERS
DeLuxe SPECIAL
Chancellor
Flavour

DIET
GRISTLE

WARMDOGS
They're
Nearly
Fresh

Two hours later the Chancellor was being converted into a carton of Export Burgers on its way to western Europe, and the King summoned his new chancellor to the throne room.

'I have a new plan,' he told the Chancellor. 'I want you to issue a Royal Proclamation.'

'Yes, sire,' said the new Chancellor.

'Everyone in the land is to fry six big onions and boil ten brussels sprouts[14] and eat them with a can of baked beans. Then at midnight, everyone must go to the lavatory. At fifteen minutes past midnight, I will drop a lighted firework down the drains.'

'Brilliant plan, oh great and wise and seriously, totally clever King of the world,' said the new Chancellor.

'Yes, it is, isn't it?' said the King, 'That should flush them out!'

'Oh, good one, sire,' laughed the Chancellor. 'Only someone as wise as yourself could have come

---

[14] *Have you ever wondered why these strange dwarf cabbages are named after the capital of Belgium? No, neither have I.*

up with such a clever plan and then been witty enough to make a joke about it.'

'Joke? What joke?' said the King.

'I will organise the decree,' said the Chancellor, hurrying away before the King realised that the explosion would probably kill everyone in the drains, including Mordonna.

'And I will go and tell the Queen about my brilliant plan,' said the King. 'She'll be so happy to get our daughter back.'

'I have a brilliant plan,' said the King, bursting into Queen Scratchrot's bedroom. 'I know I have fifty brilliant plans every day, but this is my best one ever. Our poor kidnapped daughter will be back here within the hour and Prince Nochyn will be here tomorrow for the happiest day of their lives.'

The Queen tried to push the bag she had been

packing under her bed, but the King was so excited he didn't even notice. He was so full of himself, he wasn't even aware that the Queen was wearing her riding boots or that Vessel was carrying a rucksack full of sandwiches and stay-fresh biscuits.

'She hasn't been kidnapped. I have spoken … er, I have *heard* they are in love,' said the Queen. 'She's going to marry this man.'

'I absolutely forbid it,' said the King. 'And if he so much as kisses her little finger, I will have him turned into a wood louse.'

'If you do the slightest bad thing to that lovely boy … I mean, I hear he's a lovely boy … or I, er, imagine he is or our daughter wouldn't have chosen him,' said the Queen, 'I will turn you into a one-legged rat with extra scabies and pus-filled ears.'

'Really?' said the King, intrigued.

'You wouldn't like it,' the Queen warned. 'Your ears will be filled with boiling hot bubbling pus and the only sounds you will hear will be the ten worst Eurovision Song Contest songs of all time.'

The King looked grumpy but said nothing. He knew the Queen had far more magic than he did. Slamming the door behind him, he went up to his Sulking Tower and made himself feel better by trapping hermit crabs inside their shells with waterproof sticky tape.

The Queen knew that no matter how much she threatened him and no matter what magic she did, the King would never agree to the marriage. She couldn't tell him that the lovers were already married. Even if the King didn't kill Nerlin himself, he had plenty of villains languishing in his gaols who would do it for a pair of well-fitting tights and a royal pardon. There were even desperate characters who would do it for a pair of badly fitting tights and a jar of muddy water.

There were others, of course, who thought Mordonna and Nerlin should be together – people who thought love was more important than snobbery, social standing, gold sovereigns and designer tights – but most of them kept quiet.

They had no desire to learn to water-ski or become export burgers.

'Go and warn the Dirt People,' the Queen instructed Vessel. 'Tell them to come up into the castle cellars until the explosions have finished, and tell my daughter and her lovely husband that we must flee immediately. I will meet you all by

the Friday the Thirteenth Kitchen dustbins in one hour.'[15]

'I am your Vessel, oh great wonderfulness,' said Vessel with stars and several small planets in his eyes, which made him forget there is no such word as wonderfulness. He made his way back to the drains, his heart overflowing with happiness.

The Queen packed the last few royal things into her bag and slipped down the back stairs to the stables to fetch her trusted donkey, George-The-Donkey-Formerly-Known-As-Prince-Kevin-Of-Assisi. George had seen better days. He'd seen worse days, too, and when the Queen told him they were going to flee the country, he knew that this was probably going to be one of the worse days.

---

[15] *Transylvania Waters Castle is so big that there are over eighty-seven kitchens. Apart from the obvious Monday, Tuesday, Wednesday, etc, kitchens that lots of people have, there are Christmas kitchens and kitchens for all the other special holidays like Blood-Letting Day. There are kitchens where special foods like vampire bat bladders are cooked and there are superstitious kitchens like the Friday the Thirteenth Kitchen.*

'I don't like it,' he said.[16]

'You don't like anything,' said the Queen.

'That's not true,' said George.

'OK then,' said the Queen. 'Name ten things you like.'

'Grass,' said George. 'I like grass.'

'Yes? And …'

'I'm thinking,' said George. 'Did I say grass?'

'Yes. Now stop complaining and come with me.'

The Queen put a saddle on the donkey and led him over to the kitchen dustbins. Midnight came and the air was filled with the sound of hundreds of toilets being flushed. As the clock ticked towards a quarter past, the kitchen door opened and Nerlin, Mordonna and Vessel appeared.

---

[16] *It should be pointed out here that George had actually been Prince Kevin of Assisi and had been turned into a donkey by an ancestor of Queen Scratchrot, who had needed something to carry large amounts of gold he had stolen from El Banco Nationale of Assisi. George was to all intents and purposes a real donkey, except that he could still talk. 'I don't like it' was his favourite phrase.*

'Everyone is hiding in the cellars,' said Vessel. 'They'll go back after the explos–'

The ground shook with an incredible boom, cutting off the rest of his words. The drains were

deserted as the explosion ricocheted off the walls, flinging some very unpleasant substances all over the place. Above the ground, twenty-seven people who hadn't managed to 'go' despite the baked beans,

and had still been sitting on their toilets when the explosion had detonated, all managed to 'go' very suddenly.

As people rushed to and fro with fire hoses and

sticking plasters, Vessel led the Queen on George's back and the newlyweds through the back streets towards the forest.

'My true and faithful friend, I must leave

you now,' said Mordonna to Leach, who had been waiting patiently on top of the castle wall for his mistress to reappear from the drains. 'The Himalayas are no place for a vulture with a bad neck.'

'Oh mistress, I cannot bear to see you go,' croaked the old bird. 'Without you to live for, I shall sit in a high tree and eat dead things.'

'Umm, you do that already, actually,' said Mordonna.

'So I do,' said Leach, feeling instantly better.

'Listen, old bird,' said Vessel. 'Make your way to Patagonia. All witches and wizards pass through Patagonia at least once in their life, and so it must be that we will be there one day.'

'Yes, my friend,' said Mordonna. 'To stay here would be bad for your health. I fear my father would teach you scuba diving in Lake Tarnish.'

The vulture flew back into town to find someone who could tell him what a Patagonia was, and the rest of the party walked into the forest.

'Before we leave our beloved Transylvania Waters, my lady, we must go and consult the Sheman. Such a dangerous journey as ours needs all the help it can get,' said Vessel.

'True, my wise friend,' said the Queen. 'The Sheman ... it's many years since I heard that name.'

'Don't you mean Shaman?' asked Nerlin.

'No. A Shaman is a man. A Sheman is a woman,' the Queen explained.

'I've never heard of her,' said Mordonna.

'Hardly anyone has nowadays,' said the Queen. 'King Grumpyguts made it illegal to even think about her.'

'Why?'

'He's jealous of anyone who's cleverer than him,' said the Queen. 'Which is just about everyone.

Even Snortpic the toilet seat cleaner is brighter than our glorious leader.' Patting Mordonna on the shoulder, she added, 'I thank the Lords of Darkness every day that you inherited my brains and not his.'

'So do I, Mother. Where do we find this Sheman?' said Mordonna.

'Up in the mountains,' said Vessel.

'Wow,' said Nerlin, thinking it was time he added something to the conversation.

'As you say, young master, wow,' said Vessel.

They picked their way through the forest in silence, which was only broken from time to time by George telling them he didn't like it. The lights of the town far below grew fainter and fainter until, finally, they came out above the trees onto a small plateau. Half the mountain still towered above them, glowing like a giant sapphire in the moonlight.

'We will rest here awhile,' said Vessel, who seemed to have taken charge of things.

'I wonder if we will ever see our homes again,'

said Nerlin. 'Though I'm not sure if I want to see mine again.'

'Of course we will, young master,' said Vessel. 'Even the King cannot live forever.'

'He's spiteful enough to have a go at it,' said the Queen.

After they had rested, Vessel led them along the foot of the sheer rock face until they reached a small group of bushes. Behind the bushes there was a narrow gap in the rocks that led into a steep gully. It was hard going as the moonlight couldn't reach into the gully and they were picking their way over fallen rocks in almost total darkness.

George didn't like it and told them so. The Queen dug her heels into him and he didn't like that either.

'If you don't stop complaining,' said the Queen, 'I'll strike you dumb.'

'Typical royalty,' George muttered, 'oppressing the masses.'

At the top of the gully there was a dark tunnel, but before they went in, Nerlin said, 'Why don't we

roll rocks down the gully so no one can follow us?'

'Brilliant,' said Mordonna, looking at her new husband adoringly. But Vessel held up his hand and shook his head.

'It is, as you say, young mistress, brilliant, but there will be others who will wish to escape your father's wrath in the years to come and we cannot close the way to them. Come, the Valley of the Sages and Other Herbs is through this tunnel. There are spells that will protect us once we reach it, so we must not delay.'

4

Meanwhile . . .

'GONE!' screamed the King. 'What do you mean, gone?'

'Th-th-they have f-f-f-f-f-fled, oh g-g-great one,' whimpered the Chancellor as gently as possible from inside his protective lead suit. 'It seems that your p-p-plan was not as effective as you might have hoped, sire.'

'Fetch the Queen,' the King ordered.

'Sh-sh-she has gone too, sire.'

'Don't be ridiculous,' said the King, calming down a bit. 'She can't have gone. She wouldn't leave me. Find her manservant – that creepy Vessel – and his stupid bird. He'll know where she is.'

But the more he spoke, the weaker his voice got as he realised the Queen wouldn't think twice about leaving him. In fact, she had probably thought about it a lot more times than twice, and really, it was quite amazing she hadn't gone a long time ago.

'I have had another look already, sire, and another-another look. Vessel and Parsnip are gone, and so is George-The-Donkey-Formerly-Known-As-Prince-Kevin-Of-Assisi.'

For the first time in his life the King was at a loss for words. When bad stuff happened he usually exploded, chopped a few people's heads off, laughed at a few whippets and did a mean magic trick that made everyone in the room's tights go all baggy and lumpy. After that he usually felt better. But now he was speechless.

'They were seen, sire,' said the Chancellor. 'They went into the forest.'

'Well, burn the forest to the ground,' said the King.

'Er ... sire, with most humble respect, I don't

think that's possible.' The Chancellor knew there was no way the forest would ever catch fire, not even with a whole pile of newspapers and firelighters and lightning, because the weather in Transylvania Waters was always damp. The air was filled with a drizzle that soaked everything right through without ever raining properly.[17] Most of the population had mould growing in every nook and cranny of their bodies.[18]

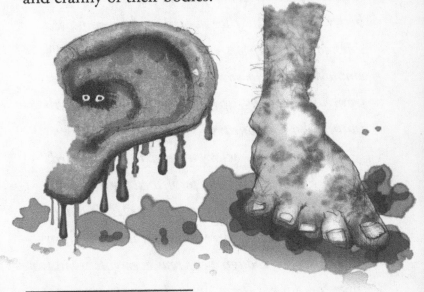

---

[17] *Like Great Britain only worse.*
[18] *A pink skin-coloured slug – The Transylvanian Misery – had evolved just to eat that mould.*

Suspecting that his previous statement could make him vulnerable to a brief bout of water-skiing, the Chancellor came up with an alternative. 'Might I suggest, sire, that you employ the best spies in the kingdom to find them instead?'

Being a spy was a very popular profession in Transylvania Waters. People were constantly suspicious that everyone else was having a better time than they were, so they employed spies to check up on each other. Even the spies employed spies to spy on the other spies. Apart from undertaking, spying was the only growth industry in the country.

Each year a directory of spies was published. No one knew exactly who published the directory. It just appeared on all the newsagents' doorsteps one morning. Spies were given a star rating from zero to seven, though very few ever got beyond three or four. There was, however, one spy company that had achieved the legendary seven star rating: Cliché, Stain & Ooze.

The three spies were in actual fact totally useless. A few spies tried to find out who published the directory so they could complain to them about the star rating system, but then they realised it could be to their advantage to have such useless spies thought of as brilliant. It meant that if they were sent after you for some reason or other, there was almost no chance they'd ever find you.

'I've just thought of the most brilliant plan,' said the King. 'Find me the names of the best spies in the kingdom.'

'I have the directory right here, sire,' said the Chancellor smoothly. 'It seems that Cliché, Stain & Ooze are the best in the land.'

'Prove it,' said the King.

The Chancellor read the King the three spies' profiles from the directory. Although they were useless, Cliché, Stain and Ooze were three of the meanest, most devious spies in a country full of useless, mean, devious spies. Cliché had sold his own grandmother for three groats to buy a rock to

throw at his grandfather. Stain had sold someone else's grandmother for two groats to buy some dust to rub in his mother's eyes, and Ooze had eaten Cliché's grandmother and Stain's mother and then framed his own father for the crime. There had been a fourth partner – Patricia – but what happened to him is far too terrible to write about. There was a dreadful smell in the street for several weeks after he vanished and Cliché, Stain and Ooze all had to have their teeth re-sharpened.

'They sound perfect. Take me to them immediately,' said the King.

Although there were only seven buildings in the street, the narrow dead-end lane where the spies had their offices was called The Street of A Thousand Doors. It was no more than twenty-three metres long, and was overshadowed by leaning walls that never let the sun reach in. It was the sort of street you only went to if you had a reason, not the sort of street that a casual visitor would ever visit. This was the street where the very best spies had their offices.

The Chancellor checked the address in the spy directory then walked up The Street of A Thousand Doors, pondering the fact that there weren't really that many doors. He waited for the King to buy a freshly roasted lizard from a greasy street vendor, then knocked on a narrow door at the very end of the street, hidden in a dark corner behind a dustbin.

Cliché, Stain & Ooze

was scratched into the red mould that crawled slowly down the woodwork.

The door opened and the two men were ushered into the spies' office. It was exactly like every private eye's office in those old-fashioned black and white movies. Everything – the floor, the walls, the furniture and the three spies – was brown and shiny and covered in sticky dust and dead flies. Each spy sat at a desk piled high with unpaid bills. Each was pretending to be very busy, but if you looked closely you could see there was a network of cobwebs over everything and a damp smell that said they hadn't had a customer for months. One feeble light bulb cast a gloomy glow that couldn't even be bothered to reach the corners of the room.

While the King sucked the insides out of his lizard, the Chancellor told the three spies their mission.

'His majesty would like his daughter back totally unharmed and his wife slightly unharmed. However, you are free to kill Nerlin and the Queen's treacherous servant,' he said. 'And if you kill the Sheman too, there will be a bonus.'

'And the donkey?' Stain asked.

'You are free to eat it,' said the Chancellor. 'In fact, I have an excellent donkey cookbook you can borrow.'

'What about our fee?' said Ooze.

'What about it?' said the King, who was flat broke. 'Am I not your King? Could you doubt that you would not get your fee? Complete this mission and you will have wealth beyond your wildest dreams.'

'Sire, there is absolutely *nothing* beyond my wildest dreams,' said Cliché. 'They are at the very limits of your imagination.'

'So could we have a deposit?' Stain asked. 'We'll have expenses to meet.'

'Yes, well, of course, exactly,' said the King. 'As soon as you get back, I will give you a deposit.'

'But sire, it's standard practice to get a deposit *before* we start,' said Ooze.

'Standard practice?' said the King. 'The King is the one who decides what is standard practice. Off you go now. There is no time to lose. The Chancellor and I will lock up for you.'

75

Cliché, Stain and Ooze knew the King's reputation and realised they were getting very close to the limit of the King's patience. They picked up their spying equipment and set off for the forest.

'Did you bring my metal detector?' said the King after the spies were out of sight.

'Yes, sire,' said the Chancellor.

'Switch it to gold detecting and search the place.'

Ten minutes later, the King was looking quite pleased with himself. 'Seven hundred and fifty-three gold sovereigns. Not bad,' he said. 'Now run after the spies and give them three sovereigns as their deposit. I'm off to the garden gnome shop.'

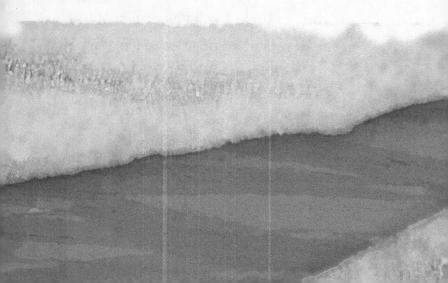

The Valley of the Sages

The newlyweds and other runaways picked their way along the dark tunnel until a faint glow appeared in the distance. The glow became a light and finally the light led into the Valley of the Sages and Other Herbs.

Although it had been the middle of the night when they had entered the tunnel an hour earlier, they had come out into broad daylight — the daylight of a summer evening that filled the magical valley twenty-four hours a day. A gentle path took them through a meadow of the softest grass speckled with mountain poppies to a stream of crystal-clear water spanned by a bridge of pure

amethyst. On the far side of the stream, the path led up through an orchard of perfect fruit and on to the sacred caves where the hermits and shamans had once lived. They were all deserted now apart from the last cave, which was home to the only person left in the valley – the Sheman.

'I *do* like it,' said George for the first time in his life. The others had to agree.

The Sheman was sitting on a chair outside her cave and didn't seem the slightest bit surprised to see them. It may seem impossible to believe but she was probably even more beautiful than Mordonna. However, her immense beauty was shrouded in an air of great sadness, for she was immortal and this created an invisible barrier between her and everyone else. Those who fell in love with her could only do so from a great distance — usually Hasselt, a town in Belgium. To come closer only ended in a broken heart, for to hear the Sheman's voice, with its deep enchanting echoes of caramel and milk chocolate, was to love her forever.

Naturally our heroes were exempt from such a

reaction, Nerlin and Mordonna on account of the fact that they were in love with each other, which gave them immunity, the Queen on account of the fact that her hearing aid tuned out caramel and milk chocolate, and Vessel because he was totally besotted with the Queen. George the donkey felt his lumpy old heart flutter a bit, but he thought it was because of something he had eaten.

'I've been expecting you,' she said as they followed her into the cave.

'How did you know we were coming?' Mordonna asked.

'I am a Sheman, we know everything.'

'Everything?' said Nerlin.

'Well,' said the Sheman, 'everything except Belgian and maths.'

'So you know why we're here?' said the Queen.

'Err, umm, yes, absolutely,' said the Sheman. 'You have come to consult me and, umm, partake of my endless wisdom.'

'Yes, sort of,' said the Queen.

'We have to flee Transylvania Waters,' said Vessel.

'In that case, we must make a sacrifice on the Golden Altar of Nebula,' said the Sheman. 'But first I must invoke the protection spell.'

She went outside, raised her arms and began to chant. The sun stopped shining and the sky grew dark. The air grew cool and it began to snow, gentle flakes drifting down in total silence, but then the wind began to blow and the snow became a blizzard.

'Hang on, did you say sacrifice?' said Nerlin. 'You're going to kill something?'

'Yes,' the Sheman explained. 'I lay the chosen creature out on the altar and chop off its head. Then I can read your future in its entrails.'

Nerlin, who had seen some pretty disgusting things in his years cleaning the drains and toilets of the city, felt faint. He was a gentle soul and the thought of killing animals upset him, especially when he was one of the reasons some poor innocent creature was going to lose its life, and doubly especially if they weren't going to eat it afterwards.

'Blood and stuff?' he said.

'Yes, that's the general idea,' said the Sheman. 'It's a great honour.'

'Who for?'

'The sacrificee, of course.'

'What, being laid out on an altar and getting your head chopped off is a great honour?'

'Oh, yes.'

'I think I'll wait outside in the nice blizzard,' said Nerlin.

'Suit yourself,' said the Sheman. After Nerlin had disappeared into the snow, she added, 'Right, now where's Nigel the sacrificial flea?'

'A flea?' said Mordonna. 'You're going to cut the head off a flea?'

'Yes.'

'You're going to stretch a flea out across the Golden Altar of Nebula and cut off its head?'

'It's a very small altar,' said the Sheman. 'Have you any idea how much gold costs? I had to use the nib off my fountain pen to make it.'

'I was kind of expecting a goat or at least a chicken.'

'Or a beautiful young woman,' Vessel added.

'Yuk,' said the Sheman. 'That's disgusting.'

'But how on Earth can you read a flea's entrails?' asked Mordonna.

'I have a very small knife and a very big magnifying glass.' She took a tiny gold altar from around her neck and something from a matchbox.

'Is it over? Only I'm getting really cold out here …' Nerlin called through the cave entrance.

'I think so,' called Mordonna.

'Oh dear, oh dear,' said the Sheman, peering at the dead flea through an enormous magnifying glass. 'I see bad omens. Dark evil forces are afoot. It will end in tears.'

'What?' said Mordonna.

'Hold on,' said the Sheman, wiping the magnifying glass on her robes. 'Oh no. I was wrong. There was a tea leaf on the lens. The omens are good. No problem. Seven children, well-fitting tights and happily ever after.'

'A tea leaf?' said Nerlin.

'Seven children?' said Mordonna. 'There goes my figure.'

6 It's a Boy

Cliché, Stain and Ooze walked across town until they stood at the edge of the forest. One of the reasons the three secret agents had seven stars was their extreme dedication to their jobs.[19] This fanatical commitment had led Stain to have himself genetically modified. He had had his nose replaced with a bloodhound's nose, which meant he could follow anyone almost anywhere simply by sniffing one of their socks.[20]

---

[19] *Another reason was that they had caused all the other possible six and seven star spies to become dead.*

[20] *I wanted to say he sniffed a pair of their undies, but this is supposed to be a children's book so I'm not allowed to.*

The Chancellor had given him one of Mordonna's eyelashes, which were normally sold in the castle gift shop for three gold sovereigns each and involved a very quiet ghost plucking them out while Mordonna was asleep.[21] They also had one of Queen Scratchrot's spare toes that she kept in a jar in the bathroom and had forgotten to pack. Cliché held the two objects to his nose and sniffed. Then he got down on all fours and sniffed some more.

'Why are you doing that?' said Stain.

'I would've thought it was obvious,' said Cliché. 'I'm trying to find where they went.'

'But we've been told they went into the forest.'

'And there's only the one path,' Ooze added.

'Well, I know,' said Cliché. 'But we might have been given false information.'

---

[21] *Don't think because the castle has a gift shop and I said there were no tourists in Transylvania Waters that I have made a mistake. The gift shop was there to supply passing citizens, who were forced inside at gunpoint and not allowed out until they had bought something.*

'We have a photo of them standing right here at the edge of the forest, and another of them just up there,' said Stain, pointing to the path.

'It could be a fake,' said Cliché. 'You can do anything with computers nowadays.'

'Go on, admit it,' said Stain. 'You just like sniffing things.'

'Especially girls' eyelashes,' sniggered Ooze.

It was a miracle that the three spies had any stars, because this was how they carried on all the time. Creeping up slowly and silently on someone was simply impossible for them. Time after time they had found the person they were looking for, crept up behind them and then given themselves away by bickering like sparrows.

'Did you bring the sandwiches?' Cliché asked as they vanished into the trees.

'I thought you were bringing the sandwiches,' said Stain.

'I brought them last time,' said Cliché.

Soon they were completely lost, which, considering there was only one path, took some doing.

Feeling safe in the Valley of the Sages and Other Herbs, with the Sheman's blizzard protecting them, the exhausted runaways decided to take the opportunity for a rest. Neurotic George was convinced he had altitude sickness and went and hid behind a tree. Even Mordonna and Nerlin, who wanted to get away as quickly as possible, agreed they would take a power-nap, which is like forty winks but half as long and with no winking.

When they woke up, the Sheman was in deep conversation with a pair of budgies.[22]

'My spies Cassandra and Clint tell me,' the Sheman reported, 'that the King has sent three secret agents after you. As we speak they are lost in the forest.'

'How can they get lost in the forest?' said Vessel. 'There's only one path.'

'I arranged to have it moved a bit,' said the Sheman.

'Shouldn't you have a creature of the night like an owl or a vampire bat spying for you?' said Mordonna. 'Budgies aren't very cool, are they?'

'Exactly,' said the Sheman. 'No one would suspect a couple of budgies flitting about. Besides, they speak a lot better than owls. I mean, have you ever tried to talk to an owl? They only know two words – 'twit' and 'twoo' – and one of *them* doesn't mean anything.'

---

[22] *Transylvanian budgies are just the same as the green Australian ones except they're black, and speak with a Transylvanian accent. They also swear a lot less than their Australian cousins.*

'Who's a pretty spy?' said one of the budgies and the pair flew off to see what the three secret agents were up to.

'As you know, there are but two roads out of Transylvania Waters – west to Transylvania and north to Russia,' said the Sheman. 'Not surprisingly, the King has posted guards at each border crossing, and on every road to the border he has secret agents bribed with offers of great wealth.'

'He doesn't have any great wealth,' said the Queen. 'He's useless, like every other king. His only talent is to squander the treasures his forefathers gathered. *I've* got all the King's gold in my handbag and teeth.'

'The common people don't know that,' said the Sheman. 'Anyway, I think this "great wealth" is more along the lines of getting to stay alive rather than getting their heads chopped off.'

'Yes, that sounds like Grumpyguts. If he gets to the end of the week without turning someone into an Export Burger he gets in a really bad mood,' said the Queen.

'Mother, he's always in a really bad mood,' said Mordonna.

'No, I mean a *really* bad mood,' said the Queen. 'He presses kittens in the pages of the seven-hundred volume Great Encyclopedia, pulls the heads off daisies, ties spiders' legs in knots and laughs at whippets with a really nasty expression on his face.'[23]

---

[23] *There is a rest home for laughed-at whippets in Transylvania Waters where the poor creatures are put on red velvet cushions and played all the Enya CDs one after the other. This wouldn't work with bulldogs, who would rather be laughed at.*

'There is one other road – though to call it a road is stretching the definition,' continued the Sheman. 'It is the route my fellow shamans and other refugees have taken to escape the King's persecution – the Sanctuary Trail. It travels east.'

'But there's just the Himalayas in the East,' said Mordonna.

'Yes, but that is your only way of escape,' the Sheman explained. 'You must go up into the mountains and through Tibet and China.'

'Can we go back and say goodbye to everyone?' Nerlin asked. 'I mean, I never said a proper leaving-the-country-forever goodbye to my mum and dad. I just said a popping-down-to-the-shops-for-a-newspaper-and-a-bag-of-lollies sort of goodbye.'

'No, you cannot go back,' said the Sheman. 'The Queen's spies tell my spies the three spies are hacking through the forest. The King has been told and has already killed two spies for failing to watch the Queen's spies. They have been beheaded and chopped into little pieces and fed to the whippets.'

'The whippets will like that,' said the Queen. 'They like minced spies.'

'You must leave now, before nightfall,' said the Sheman, 'I will send one of my budgies along to show you the way.'

'Shouldn't we wait until the blizzard has died down?' said Nerlin. 'You can hardly see your hand in front of your face out there.'

'What blizzard?' said the Sheman, clicking her fingers behind her back.

'Outside,' said Nerlin. 'It's blowing a hurricane.'

'No, I don't think so.'

Nerlin went to the front of the cave, and sure enough, there was no sign of the blizzard that had been raging a few minutes before. There wasn't even a single snowflake left. The magical daylight of a summer evening filled the valley again and George had come out from behind his tree to happily browse the perfect grass and the big red flowers.

'I don't know what's in these poppies,' he said, 'but they are delicious.'

93

'We have to go,' said the Queen.

'I might have known it,' said George. 'Soon as I get somewhere nicer than anywhere else in the world, we have to go.'

'Not that way,' said the Sheman as the donkey turned back towards the bridge. 'Follow Cassandra.'

The black budgie sat on George's head and pointed with her wing. Every time the donkey turned in the wrong direction, she pecked him and squawked. They passed six deserted shaman caves. At the seventh, the budgie perched on a twig and pointed.

'In there,' she said. 'Bye.'

'Is that it?' said Mordonna. 'I thought you were supposed to show us the way.'

'I just did,' said Cassandra and flew off.

'I don't like it,' said George. 'So it must be the right place.'

At the back of the cave a steep tunnel climbed right up into the heart of the mountain and, hours later, came out the other side. Now they *were* in

94

snow, mountains covered in the stuff for as far as the eye could see. Up here, the air was as thin and cold as a witch's broomstick.[24]

'Now I really don't like it,' said George. 'Do I look like a polar bear? I should be in fields of soft grass, not this frozen wasteland.'

'Stop moaning and watch where you're going,' snapped the Queen.

They had come out on a narrow, slippery, icy ledge above a sheer drop that disappeared into mist far below them on the right. On their left the mountain was a sheer wall of ice that disappeared into clouds above them. An eerie, mournful howling drifted down from the mountain tops.

'What is that?' said Nerlin. 'It sounds hungry.'

'That is the Abominable Snow Person,' said Vessel, 'and it is probably hungry. So would you be with nothing but abominable snow to eat.'

'Come on, George, let's go,' said the Queen.

---

[24] *Except for the bit the witch had been sitting on, which would be warm.*

95

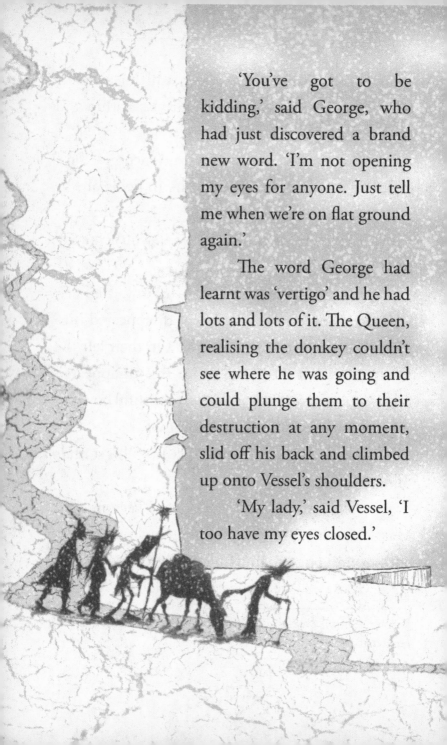

'You've got to be kidding,' said George, who had just discovered a brand new word. 'I'm not opening my eyes for anyone. Just tell me when we're on flat ground again.'

The word George had learnt was 'vertigo' and he had lots and lots of it. The Queen, realising the donkey couldn't see where he was going and could plunge them to their destruction at any moment, slid off his back and climbed up onto Vessel's shoulders.

'My lady,' said Vessel, 'I too have my eyes closed.'

'Oh, for goodness sake, the pair of you, just don't faint whatever you do,' said the Queen, climbing down. 'Vessel, you hold the donkey's tail and I'll pull it along by its left ear.'

She led them down into the mist. Nerlin, at the back of the line, said very quietly that he felt he should really be in front as he was young and fearless. Fortunately, he said it too quietly for anyone else to hear.

As they walked, the ground cracked beneath their feet, sending huge chunks of ice and rock crashing down into the abyss. As they entered the mist the path got wider and the howling grew fainter. At last they reached the valley floor.

'You can open your eyes now,' said Mordonna. 'We're on flat ground.'

'Are you sure?' said the Queen.

'Yes, can't you see?'

'No, I had my eyes shut too.'

'So did I,' said Nerlin.

George opened his eyes and groaned.

'Yeah, yeah, we know,' said Nerlin. 'You don't like it. Well, join the party.'

'Listen, everyone. I don't want to make a fuss or anything,' said Mordonna, 'but I'm going to have a baby.'

'Congratulations, my lady,' said Vessel. 'The Sheman's predictions are coming to pass.' Turning to the Queen, he added, 'Is it not wonderful, my great and glorious queen? Is it not just like Romeo and Juliet? Is it not just like *West Side Story*? Is it not just like Barry and Isolda?'

The Queen patted him on the arm and put her arms round Mordonna.

'I thought you had put on a bit of weight, darling,' said the Queen, 'but I didn't say anything in case it was just a thick vest.'

'No, mother, it's a baby,' said Mordonna, 'and I should say that not only am I going to have a baby, I'm actually going to have it very shortly.'

'But …' Nerlin began. He had been given the standard Dirt People education about babies, where they came from (a Special Shop), how to

decide if you wanted a boy or a girl (wear red or blue socks), and how long it all took (more than boiling an egg, but less than going to Belgium and buying a cardigan). 'When did you go to the Special Shop?'

'My darling, I'm a witch and a princess, remember?' Mordonna explained. 'I don't have to go to the Special Shop and I don't have to waste lots of time being sick in the morning and having backache. I just used the Special Princess-Witch Hurry-Up Spell so the whole thing only takes twenty-four hours.'

'Right,' said the Queen, taking charge. 'We need towels and hot water.'

'We're in the remotest part of the Himalayas,' said Nerlin, lifting Mordonna onto George's back. 'I'm guessing it's not a big towel and hot water area.'

'Follow me,' said Vessel, walking down the valley.

'Where?' said Nerlin.

'There's a stable just round the next corner

with a very comfortable manger and hot food and even soft hay for the ungrateful donkey,' Vessel's voice said out of the mist.

'What?' said Nerlin, running after the equery. 'You've got to be kidding.'

'I am not without some considerable magical powers myself, you know,' said Vessel. 'And it's your wife who is "kidding", as she is just about to have a kid, ha, ha.'

They rounded a massive block of ice and there, exactly as Vessel had predicted, was a stable, complete with a comfy manger, a full kettle boiling away on the stove, a huge pile of soft fluffy towels and a table groaning with food, though the coffee and blood were only instant and not fresh as everyone would have preferred.

'The manger's a bit small,' said Mordonna, who was entitled to complain because she was about to have a baby any minute. 'I'll never fit in it and it looks like it'll fall off the wall.'

'It's for the baby, not you,' the Queen explained.

'Oh,' said Mordonna.

Everyone used the boiling water to have a cup of instant coffee.

Five minutes later Mordonna said, 'So what are we going to call him?'

'How do you know it's a boy?' said Nerlin.

'Well, look,' Mordonna replied, holding up what appeared to be a large wrinkled prune with very white skin. 'Say hello to your son.'

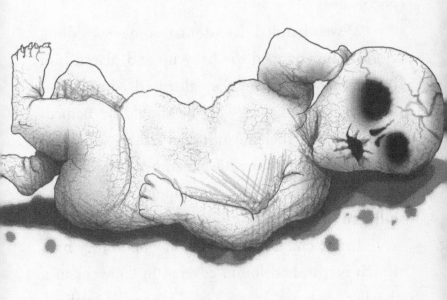

'Er, hello,' said Nerlin.

'Hello, Daddy,' said the baby.

Normal babies don't speak until they are a lot older than several minutes, but this was not a normal baby. This baby was not even a normal wizard. This baby was the child of a powerful princess-witch and a direct descendant of the great Merlin. He wasn't about to waste several years wetting nappies, throwing up over his mother's shoulder and grinning inanely at stuffed toys with googly eyes.

Vessel handed Mordonna some swaddling cloths. She wrapped the baby up and placed him in the manger, where they all gazed adoringly at him and argued over what he should be named. Everyone had their favourites. Parsnip wanted to name him Turnip after his father. Nerlin wanted to call him Walter and George thought they should call him George.

In the end they took the only book they had, which Nerlin had found covered in cobwebs in a derelict bookcase. It was a road atlas of Australia.

Nerlin closed his eyes, stuck his finger between the pages and opened the book.

'Valla,' he said. 'We shall call him Valla.'

'I like it,' said Valla. Everyone agreed except George, who let them know he didn't like it.

'Valla's probably hungry,' said Nerlin, trying to be a responsible dad.

'Yes, of course, brilliant idea, darling. What do you think he'd like?' Mordonna asked.

'Well, er, milk, of course,' said Nerlin. 'Isn't that what all newborn babies have?'

'Not necessarily,' said the Queen. 'You must remember this baby is a wizard and wizards often eat different things to humans.'

They tried milk, then strawberry jam, then melted Tim Tams, but Valla spat them all out. They tried a banana, but the baby clamped his mouth shut before they could get near him. Mordonna started peeling an apple. As she did, she cut her finger. Three drops of blood splashed into baby Valla's mouth and he roared with delight. His eyes sparkled and his tongue licked round his lips to get every last drop.

'Now you're talking,' said Valla. 'More blood, Mum!'

'Blood, of course!' said the Queen. 'I should have known … he takes after his great-grandfather. The similarity is uncanny, the black rings round the dark sunken eyes and skin so white that it's almost transparent. He may only be a baby but he's Great-Grandfather Formaldehyde to a T. He'll have the girls falling at his feet.'[25]

Later on when everyone was asleep, the Queen whispered in Vessel's ear, 'I've never seen a bookcase in a stable before.'

---

[25] *Great-Grandfather Formaldehyde had the girls falling at his feet too, mostly because they fainted in horror when they saw him.*

'No, my lady, neither have I,' said Vessel. 'Strange, isn't it?'

'You cunning old fox,' said the Queen. 'And what a strange choice of book.'

She moved closer to the equery. 'It's very cold in here, isn't it?' she whispered so as not to wake Mordonna and Nerlin.

'Yes, my lady.'

'I imagine we would both feel warmer if we sat closer to each other.'

'Undoubtedly, my lady,' said Vessel feeling excited, scared, lightheaded, giddy, wobbly, woozy, shaky and happy all at the same time.

He leaned his staff against the wall and put his arm round the Queen's bony shoulder. He was happier than he had ever been in his whole life.

'And how strange that all the pages in the book were stuck together except that particular one,' murmured the Queen.

'Indeed.'

'And even stranger that all the place names were blotted out except the one – Valla.'

105

'Strange doesn't even come close,' said Vessel.

'There's more to you than meets the eye, Vessel. By the way, what's your first name?' asked the Queen.

'I don't know,' said Vessel. 'I have two initials but no one ever told me what they stood for.'

'Initials?'

'Yes. M.T. My father always called me M.T. Vessel.'

'Then I shall call you M, but you must call me Scratchie, though in public we should probably keep calling each other "Vessel" and "Your Majesty", at least for the moment,' said the Queen. 'Now, M, your queen orders you to kiss her.'

Vessel's false teeth fell out into the straw and he fainted.

Parsnip, in his nest leaning against the wall, cursed under his breath. Where was the love of *his* life, then? No one ever thought of him, did they? He made up his mind that as soon as they got somewhere warmer, he was off. He'd told himself a million times before that he would leave, but when

it had come to it he hadn't been able to. After all, Vessel was the closest thing he had ever had to a mum or dad. Vessel had rescued him as an egg from the wreckage of his parents' nest and had incubated him under his left armpit.

Not many crows could say that.

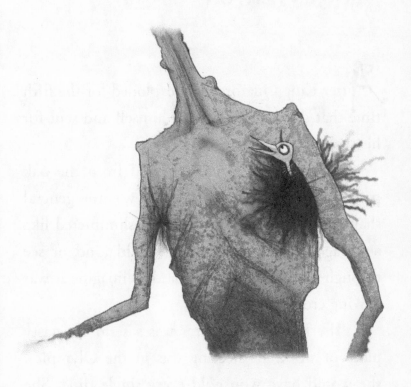

The Hearse Whisperer

After King Quatorze had exploded for the fifth time that day he reassembled himself and sent for his secret, secret agent.

An indistinct figure emerged from the oak panelling that lined the room. It was the general shape and size of a person, but it shimmered like a mirage, a dark mirage you could kind of see through like smoke. It was hard to imagine it was a living creature.

The Hearse Whisperer was a seriously nasty piece of work. If sneering was in the Olympics, she would have won gold every single time. She looked down her nose at everything and everyone.

She had had her own parents locked up in jail for being too kind to her, which she claimed in court had threatened her future survival.

'How can I be expected to get on in life if I am nice to people?' she had said to the judge. 'Look at my parents, two disgustingly nice laid-back hippies, and see where being nice has got them.'

'Where?' asked the judge.

'Nowhere,' sneered the Hearse Whisperer. 'They drive a kombi van with rainbows painted on the doors and they share their bedroom with chickens.'

'You're absolutely right,' the judge agreed, and for their excessive kindness he sentenced the Hearse Whisperer's parents to a lifetime in Transylvania Waters' maximum security jail, Howlcatraz, which was on an island in Lake Tarnish.[26]

---

[26] *On Howlcatraz the Hearse Whisperer's parents were happier than they had ever been. They organised a gardening club and a folk club and a soya-bean embroidery club. Every time there was any talk of them getting parole and being sent home, they got drunk on gooseberry wine and smashed a few windows to ensure they were kept there.*

If you had been able to see the Hearse Whisperer clearly, you would have noticed that every part of her was pointed. Her nose, which she poked into everything, could break glass, and if she had been any thinner she could have got a job as a bookmark. She was known around town as the stick insect, and although no one ever dared call her that to her face, she knew. She had seen the graffiti.

People said that underneath her mean, sarcastic exterior, there was just a little girl looking for love, but there wasn't. Underneath her mean, sarcastic exterior, there was something far worse, something too foul to survive in daylight.

'I have a mission for you,' said the King. 'A mission that will require all your cunning and deceit and all your brilliant body-changing magic.'

'You want me to find the princess,' said the Hearse Whisperer in a voice that sounded like three rough rocks tied to a bit of string being pulled down the throat of a very, very old man.

'Exactly. Once again you have read my thoughts.'

Not too difficult, thought the secret, secret agent. *I could read your whole pathetic little mind in fifteen seconds and still have time to make a cup of tea.*

The Hearse Whisperer occupied a unique place in the King's household. Apart from the Queen, she was the only person who the King had never threatened to have killed. This was because

she always got the results he wanted and was totally devoted to the King. At least, that's what he told himself. The truth was that he was scared of her, same as he was scared of the Queen.

Not only was the Hearse Whisperer a secret, secret agent, but her life itself was a secret secret. No one knew when or where she would appear and in what form, or where she went at night, or what went on inside her head or which one of the Skeletals was her favourite.[27] She was the King's favourite secret agent because she never asked him for any wages. She just did it from the sheer love of causing distress to as many people as possible.[28]

'As you know I hired our country's top spies – Cliché, Stain and Ooze – to follow the princess and her abductor.'

---

[27] *The Skeletals – Gorge, Prowl, Stinko and Beryl – were Transylvania Waters' most famous pop group. In fact, they were Transylvania Waters's only pop group. The Hearse Whisperer, of course, hated them all.*
[28] *Of course she could have caused even more distress by becoming a physics teacher, but they didn't have them in Transylvania Waters' schools.*

'I do, sire,' said the Hearse Whisperer, well aware how useless the three spies were. 'I know too that the Queen, her vile servant and her stupid donkey have fled with them.'

'Exactly. And I suspect that foul Sheman has confused the path through the forest so the three spies keep ending up back here in town,' said the King. 'I want you to undo this magic and guide them through the forest, but make sure they don't know you're there because I want you to follow them, and when they have led you to my daughter I want you to kill them, and all the others except my daughter. And as a reward you can kill them in the most painful way you can think of.'

'And the Queen?'

'Kill her too,' said the King, rubbing his chubby fingers together. 'It's time I got a new one.'

'No problem,' said the Hearse Whisperer, turning into a pigeon.

'Report back to me with any news,' said the King. 'I suspect those spies will sell their services to the highest bidder.'

113

'Perhaps, sire, you should have given them more than three sovereigns' deposit,' said the Hearse Whisperer.

'How did you know that?'

'You probably did not notice the small slug crawling up the fifteenth leaf of the deadly nightshade plant in the flowerpot on the windowsill in Cliché, Stain and Ooze's office,' the Hearse Whisperer explained. 'That was me.'

'What were you doing there?' asked the King.

'As always, sire, I was protecting you,' said the Hearse Whisperer and flew out of the window.

She floated over the rooftops towards the forest, setting the odd line of washing on fire just to keep her hand in. This was no mean feat considering the perpetual dampness everywhere.[29]

---

[29] *Just to illustrate how dull, damp and totally crap the weather is in Transylvania Waters, the weather forecast was recorded fifty years ago and has been played on TV every night since then. Basically, an old wizard points at a grey sheet of paper and says: 'That's tomorrow's weather. It could brighten up by the weekend but probably won't.'*

Unseen by anyone below, she drifted over the forest. She was in no hurry. Time was on her side – though if time had realised just how deeply evil she was, it would have had nothing to do with her. As it was, it simply stood still for her, allowing her to remain the same for century after century. The Hearse Whisperer had served the King's father and his grandfather and back until the first of the line had risen up and driven Nerlin's ancestors into the

drains to live as the wretched Dirt People. She had played no small part in that revolution, though most people were completely unaware of her existence. Most people thought the Hearse Whisperer was a legend, an invention parents could use to scare their children when they were being naughty.

When she found Cliché, Stain and Ooze, they were walking in such small circles that they were following themselves. The Hearse Whisperer ignored them. They would eventually make their way into the Valley of the Sages and Other Herbs but, by the time they did, Nerlin and Mordonna would probably be grandparents. A black budgie was circling the spies, squawking swear words at them.

'Ah, the Sheman's little helper. Come here, tasty morsel,' the Hearse Whisperer whispered. She set the bird's feathers alight and it flew straight into a tree trunk at the edge of the forest, where the Hearse Whisperer was waiting for it. She picked it up, put out its burning wings and held it close to her face.

'Tell me, little snack food … tell me where they are.'

'Drop dead,' said Cassandra, for it was she, and not her partner, Clint.

'Wrong answer,' said the Hearse Whisperer, resisting the urge to fry the budgie to a crisp.[30] 'Tell me or I will clip your wings.'

'Never,' said Cassandra.

'I don't mean clip your wings,' said the Hearse Whisperer, correcting herself. 'I mean clip your wings *off*.'

In her cave, the Sheman sensed the presence of the Hearse Whisperer and knew that one of her two budgies was in trouble. She knew that if she sent Clint out to see what was happening, the Hearse Whisperer would take him too. She sat cross-legged on the ground and sent her mind out into Cassandra's.

'Ah, your mistress has decided to join us,' said the Hearse Whisperer. 'So we meet again, Sheman.

---

[30] *Budgie-flavoured crisps are the most popular flavour in Transylvania Waters.*

Last time we met you caught me off-guard because I was so jealous of your staggering beauty, but now we are enemies. This time I shall destroy you.'

Run For It

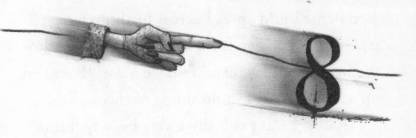

I n the Himalayas the mist had lifted and the sun shone down into a two-coloured world. Above, the sky was a bright clear blue. Everything else was covered in a layer of fresh white snow that had fallen during the night. It was as if no living creature had ever set foot in this high valley. The stable itself was almost hidden beneath a large snowdrift.

Inside the stable the air was warm and humid, filled with the sweet smell of damp hay. Baby Valla lay in his manger, gurgling quietly to himself as he sucked his thumb. Being a wizard, with a touch of vampire from his great-great-grandfather on his mother's side, he already had tiny fangs, and

soon punctured his own skin. This would make a human baby cry, but as Valla tasted his own blood, a contented grin spread across his little face. His parents lay together, half buried in the straw below the manger, and across the stable Vessel lay curled up at the Queen's feet dreaming of cheese.

George was gradually eating his way through the Queen's bed when she woke with a shudder and sat up.

'What is it, my queen?' said Vessel. 'Are you cold?'

'Go on, blame it on me,' George whinged. 'Can't even eat a bit of breakfast without someone complaining.'

'No, it's not the cold,' said the Queen. 'I felt the icy hand of death on my shoulder. The Hearse Whisperer comes behind us and she is one who will never rest until she has found us.'

'The Hearse Whisperer?' said Nerlin. 'My grandfather used to speak of her, but none of us believed she was real.'

'We must leave,' said the Queen. 'The further

120

away we get, the better. I knew the King would send people after us, but I never thought he would use someone as evil as the Hearse Whisperer.'

'We need to find some food for our new baby,' said Mordonna. 'I know puncturing your own veins is a great way to keep a deadly pale complexion, but I'd rather not.'

'Blood, blood, blood,' gurgled Valla.

'Oh bless him,' said the Queen. 'Look at that blood round his little mouth. What an angel.'

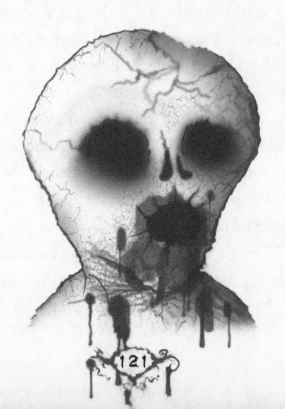

'Who's mummy's little vampire?' said Mordonna fondly as baby Valla sunk his fangs into her thumb. 'But, oww, oww, we really need to find him some food, like, oww, oww, as soon as possible.'

'We can get supplies from a blood bank,' said the Queen.

'Hello?' said Nerlin. 'Himalayas? I don't see any branches of Bloods R Us.'

'Oh, I don't know,' said Vessel, knowingly. 'It wouldn't surprise me if there was one up here somewhere. I mean, mountain climbers are always having accidents. I would have thought there'd be quite a demand.'

Nerlin put his son in his backpack, helped Mordonna up onto George's back and the party went out into the blinding whiteness. It almost felt like spring rather than the depths of winter, provided you were a penguin or a yeti.

'I might have known,' George moaned, 'every blade of grass is buried under tonnes of snow.'

Mountain after mountain, joined by a line of

deep valleys, lay ahead of the travellers, but just as Vessel had predicted, a mile or so past the stable there was a small wooden hut half buried in a snow drift. Above its door hung a sign:

Blood Bank
High Altitude Blends Our Specialty

'Morning, ladies and gents,' said the man behind the counter. 'What can I do for you on this bright, almost spring-like morning?'

'Sixty litres of your finest red,' said Vessel, 'to go.'

'What group?'

'All of them,' said Vessel.

'I've only got fifty-eight litres in stock,' said the shopkeeper. 'Hold on. I'll nip out the back and get some more.'

The man vanished into a room at the back of the shop and, after a few loud screams followed by

silence, he returned with two more bottles and a big bandage on his arm.

'There you go, squire,' he said. 'That'll be fifteen sovereigns.'

'Here's twenty-five,' said the Queen. 'An extra two as a tip and eight to forget you ever saw us if anyone comes asking.'

'Is someone likely to?' the man asked.

'I'm afraid so,' said Vessel, handing the man a small pill box. 'I'd advise you to take these three times a day for the next week or so.'

'What are they?'

'Heavy duty painkillers. Some of the people following us are not very nice,' said Vessel. This was an extremely huge understatement, but he knew that if told the blood bank man just how not nice they were, he would probably run away with them. 'I think we should probably hypnotise you too and do a bit of memory reformatting in your brain, just to be on the safe side,' Vessel added.

Mordonna uncapped a one-litre bag of blood and popped the nozzle into Valla's mouth. He

kicked his little legs with such excitement he nearly fell out of Nerlin's backpack.

Fifty-nine litres of blood flopping about in two saddlebags gave George something else to moan about as they set off down the valley. Gradually the snow grew thinner until at last they were below the snow line. They followed a path along a river that jumped and sparkled over bare rocks. Grass began to appear, then stunted trees and small groups of houses with people who waved as they passed.

They stopped in a village and bought food before moving on again.

'Rubbish grass,' said George. 'Tastes like mulch.'

'We really need to get off this main path,' said Vessel. 'This is the first place they will look for us.'

'What, you mean find somewhere where the grass is even crappier?' said George.

'Where exactly are we going?' said the Queen.

'Wherever it is, I bet it's somewhere bleak and cold with really tough grass,' said George.

'We're going East,' said Vessel. 'When we get to Shanghai we will find a boat. Then we'll decide where to go from there.'

'Shanghai?' said the Queen. 'How romantic. Are we going to travel along the famous Silk Road?'

'If only we could,' said Vessel. 'But the King will have spies all along that road. No, we will take the older and lesser-known road, the Cardboard Road.'

The Cardboard Road was an ancient route where traders had carried cardboard from the workshops of China to the cities of Europe. It had only existed for two hundred years before the Europeans had managed to analyse and successfully copy the Chinese cardboard and make cardboard of their own. There had also been a Porridge Road, where traders had carried porridge from its place of origin – a small town on a ridge above the River Po – to England. It had only taken British scientists eighty years to isolate the main ingredient – oats – and a further fifty years to discover the other ingredient – water. After that the Porridge Road, along with the Lard Road, the Soap Road and the Yellow Brick Road Road, had fallen into disuse and vanished beneath encroaching vegetation. Nowadays the only road that still operates is the I Can't Believe It's Not Butter Road.

Eventually, after three days of hacking through undergrowth, following themselves, setting traps for and catching each other, Cliché, Stain and Ooze reached the Valley of the Sages and Other Herbs. The first thing they saw was the Hearse Whisperer sitting on a rock filing her nails.

'You three couldn't follow your own fingers if they were on the ends of your hands and were pointing where you had to go,' she said.

The three spies, who hadn't the faintest idea that the Hearse Whisperer was the King's secret, secret agent, tried to ignore her, but as they walked past she put out her foot and tripped the first one, sending the other two crashing down on top of him.

'Oops,' she said. 'Now why don't you just go back home and get killed by the King? You are the crappiest spies in the whole history of spying and you couldn't find a snowflake in a blizzard, never mind catch a princess, her husband, her mother, the mother's servant and a donkey.'

'How do you know about that?' said Cliché.

'Assuming that's what we are doing, of course,' Stain added hastily. 'Which we're not.'

'No, of course we're not,' said Ooze. 'We don't know what you're talking about. We're just doing a bit of hiking.'

'Oh, yes, that's right,' said Cliché. 'What princess?'

'Look, I work for the King,' said the Hearse Whisperer. The three idiots might be of some use to her, though she couldn't exactly see how. 'He sent me here to help you,' she added.

'Oh,' said Stain.

'So, you're on your way to … ?' Cliché began, hoping the Hearse Whisperer knew where they were supposed to be going.

'Yes, absolutely.'

'To see the umm, the err …' said Ooze.

'Yes.'

'Excellent,' said Stain. 'We'll follow you.'

'No, no, you lead the way,' said the Hearse Whisperer.

'Wouldn't dream of it,' said Cliché.

'Ladies first,' said Ooze.

'You don't know where you're going, do you?'

'Well, umm, err, no.'

'To find the Sheman?' prompted the Hearse Whisperer.

'We knew that,' said Ooze.

'Yes, we just wanted to make sure you really were on our side,' Stain added.

'Yeah right,' said the Hearse Whisperer. 'Come on, let's go then.'

When they reached the caves, it was obvious which one was the Sheman's as there was laundry hanging up to dry outside and a recycling bin with a takeaway lentil container and a pair of organic socks in it. It didn't take them long to realise the Sheman was not there.

'She's escaped!' the Hearse Whisperer wheezed, setting fire to the Sheman's cave in frustration.

Stain got down on all fours and began to sniff the ground.

'This way,' he said, heading towards the

cave that led to the Sanctuary Trail. They slid and tumbled down the icy mountain path until they reached the stable where Valla had been born.

'I smell new life,' said Stain sticking his head in the manger. 'Baby boy, no more than a few hours old.'

The Hearse Whisperer vented her anger by setting the manger alight. She did this a few seconds before Stain pulled his head out of the straw. The spy screamed and fell on the floor clutching his left ear. A strong smell of fried bacon filled the air.

'Excellent,' said the Hearse Whisperer. 'A child will slow them down. We'll rest here for the night and set off at dawn. We will have them in chains before lunchtime.'

China

9

Once out of the mountains, the refugees made better progress. Using ancient Buddhist Mountain Running And Leaping Skills which Vessel had learnt at his mother's knee,[31] they managed to cover huge distances in mere minutes so that by late afternoon they were having tea and cakes in Shangri-La, and by evening they had reached the Chinese border. Of course, once they crossed into China, the mystical running and leaping skills

---

[31] *Most of Vessel's mother was not terribly bright but her knee was incredibly talented and carried all the wisdom of the ancient Buddhas, including how to run really fast and cook rice without it all sticking together.*

stopped working and they were forced to travel on foot. Nevertheless, they reached the Great Wall of China Inn and Noodle Takeaway Number Seventy-Three by nightfall, just in time for a delicious meal before the kitchen closed.

Their pursuers had to make do with bicycles and a faulty broomstick that kept flying backwards. This meant that when they finally reached the Inn, it was after midnight and they were forced to eat what they could scavenge out of the dustbins.

'The Princess has been chewing this,' said Stain, sticking a chicken bone up his nose and inhaling deeply.

'So what's the plan?' said Cliché. 'Grab her and kill the rest of them?'

'It's not that simple,' said the Hearse Whisperer. 'They have very strong magic. We need to catch them off-guard.'

'They're asleep,' said Ooze. 'How much more off-guard can they get?'

'We're not all asleep,' said a gloomy voice from the shadows.

133

'Some vatch up on you from below outside in,' said another voice from the roof.

'It's just the stupid donkey and the servant's crazy bird,' whispered Stain.

'Stupid, maybe,' said George, 'but with hearing sharper than a pin and kung-fu hooves.'

The four spies agreed to wait for an unguarded moment when they would be able to strike.

Parsnip flew through his master's bedroom window and tapped him on the head.

'Four pies, master, flee now must go do,' he said.

Vessel woke everyone. The four spies were busy poking around the dustbins for food, so the refugees slipped quietly out of the front door and off into the night.

The refugees had many, many miles to travel to reach Shanghai and find a boat, but they were in

no hurry and agreed with Vessel when he said that travelling slowly would be exactly the opposite of what the King's spies would expect. So they took detours to beautiful villages and walked along country roads past gentle streams.

Time passed and everyone except Valla got five months older. Little Valla got five years older. He even went to some of the village schools, where he learnt Chinese calligraphy and how to make delicate porcelain bowls.

'Because,' he explained, 'you never know when things like that might come in handy. And besides, fresh blood looks so appetising in a fragile white bowl.'

They had to leave most of the villages in rather a hurry when Valla kept drinking blood out of the local chickens and his fellow students' necks, but each time the Queen would wave her wand and do the forget-we-were-ever-here spell, so no one came after them.

The spies did not overtake them, as Vessel had predicted, but followed at a discreet distance,

staying just one village behind them. There were many occasions when the Hearse Whisperer was sure they could have overpowered the refugees and kidnapped Mordonna, but her three pathetic companions were such dreadful cowards they always found excuses why it wasn't the right time. Even the Hearse Whisperer felt uneasy about a confrontation. She knew she could overpower Vessel, Nerlin and Mordonna on her own, but Queen Scratchrot was another story. They had crossed swords in the past and the Queen had usually come out on top. Also, only an idiot would be in a hurry to get back to Transylvania Waters and its awful king, and the Hearse Whisperer was not an idiot.

So, she waited.

At last the runaways reached the outskirts of Shanghai. One look at the group would tell anyone that they had as much chance of blending in as a glass of water in an oil slick, except that the Queen and her party were more like the oil slick in a sea of clean water.

'I think we should split up and meet at the

harbour in two hours,' said Vessel. 'That way we might not stand out so much.'

'I'm not splitting up,' said George. 'All my insides will fall out.'

'Actually, good and faithful friend ...' the Queen began.

'Uh oh, bad stuff,' said George. 'Whenever you talk like that, it's always followed by something I don't like.'

'This time you will like it,' said the Queen, 'because you are going to get a huge reward.'

'Oh yes?'

'Absolutely,' the Queen explained. 'Which would you rather do: get on a very small boat and set off into a wild and stormy sea where you are guaranteed to be horribly seasick every ten minutes, or spend the rest of your life in this lovely field we are now standing in?'

'Boat,' said George.

'No you wouldn't,' said the Queen. 'Look at all this lovely grass.'

'Don't like Chinese grass,' said George.

137

'Yes you do,' said the Queen. 'You're just being silly. Here we are offering you a life of leisure and luxury as a reward for all the hard work you have done for us, and all you can do is complain. You are a very ungrateful animal. I've half a mind to turn you into a boiled egg.'

'Go on then,' said George.

'Look, any donkey would give his right hoof to be sold to this wonderful Chinese gentleman,' said Vessel. 'Lovely fresh ditch water, all the grass you can eat and all you have to do is carry a few really tiny bags of ultra-lightweight coal out of his

lovely clean mine eighty-seven times a day.'

'Can't I be a boiled egg instead?' said George.

'No,' said the Queen.

She stared deep into the donkey's eyes and said, 'Now look, everyone knows that donkeys are the worst sailors in the world. You would be so seasick it would fill up the boat and sink it.'

'Who told you that?' said George.

'It's a well-known fact,' said Mordonna. 'Everyone knows that.'

'I don't,' said George.

'Listen, donkey, if being seasick was in the Olympic Games all the medals would be won by donkeys.'

'But, I err, umm ...' George began, but he was now so confused that the thought of coal mining was beginning to look quite appealing.

'And this lovely man is going to pay us three whole fen[32] for the honour of allowing you to carry his extra special bio-organic low-fat coal.'

---

[32] *About 0.005 Australian dollars.*

'Three fen? Is that a lot of money?' said George. 'After all, I've given you the best years of my life.'

Trouble is, you gave me the worst ones too, thought the Queen.

'Well, of course it is. You are probably the most valuable donkey in the whole world,' she said.

Before he could say another word and before the Queen could start feeling guilty, Vessel took the miner's three tiny coins and handed him George's halter. After man and donkey had disappeared into the coal mine, Nerlin said, 'Is that enough to buy a boat?'

'Not so much a boat as a very small nail to start building a boat with,' said Vessel. 'We'd need fifty billion fen to buy a whole boat. That is, if we were going to buy one.'

'So, we're not going by boat?'

'Oh yes, we are,' said Vessel, 'but we're not so much going to buy a boat as borrow one.'

Although the Queen had a big bag of gold and Mordonna had all her pockets stuffed with precious stones, and witches and wizards can always

get money by magic, Vessel only had the three fen he'd been given for George, and his male pride wouldn't let him ask the Queen or her daughter to help. Besides, as far as he was concerned they weren't going to keep the boat. They only needed it for a little while, so he didn't see why he should have to pay for it.

'You mean steal one?' said Nerlin.

'I think "steal" is such a nasty word, don't you?'

'Actually, I quite like it,' said Nerlin. 'Don't forget I grew up in the drains. We had to steal everything just to survive.'

'Ah, how true,' said Vessel, remembering his own childhood.

'Well, we'll just say we're borrowing the boat,' said the Queen. 'When we've finished with it, the owners can come and get it back.'

'Of course,' Vessel added, 'the three idiot spies hiding in the tree above our heads will probably "borrow" a boat too.'

Cliché, Stain and Ooze all began doing bird

141

impersonations to try and throw the fugitives off the scent.

'Oh, listen,' said Vessel. 'There are three pigeons up in that tree. Can't remember the last time I had pigeon pie. Where's my gun?'

Cliché, Stain and Ooze fell out of the tree and landed at Nerlin's feet. Pretending to be Belgian[33] tourists, they began babbling incoherently and bowing and backing away in the direction of the coal mine, which they fell down. They landed on George, who most definitely did not like it and told them so in several languages, including Belgian.

The Hearse Whisperer kept very still up in the branches. She really was disguised as a pigeon, and had no intention of becoming a pie.

'Oops,' said the Queen, watching George's kung-fu hooves connecting with the three spies' bottoms. 'Time to go, I think.'

---

[33] *If you are Belgian, please don't take this personally. Every time you see the word Belgian, just pretend it says 'Welsh'. If you are Welsh, don't come to me for sympathy. What do you expect if you insist on wearing silly hats with torches on?*

Nerlin and Mordonna with baby Valla went one way. The Queen and Vessel went another and Parsnip flew overhead, keeping a lookout for the spies. They blended in like barbed wire at a jellyfish party, but because they looked so weird, no one dared bother them, though several people did invite Parsnip to join them in a sweet and sour crow and noodle dinner.

The three spies didn't manage to escape from the mine until they had each carried seven bags of coal to the surface at the suggestion of the miner, who had a large stick and an angry donkey. The Hearse Whisperer had followed Vessel and the Queen down to the harbour and sat watching them from a tall chimney. She knew the Queen would sense her presence if she got too near so she kept a safe distance.

'Right,' said Vessel when he and the Queen reached the wharf, 'we need to find a boat, something big enough to survive the open sea.'

'None of these is much good,' said the Queen. 'They're a load of junk.'

144

'Very funny,' said Vessel. 'But that one at the end of the harbour looks promising. The one with the French flag.'

'How will we get everyone else off the ship?' said Nerlin, who had just reached them with Mordonna.

'No problem,' said the Queen. 'We are wizards, after all.'

She took a small wand from her sleeve and waved it at herself. There was a flash and the Queen turned into a twenty-three-year-old French cafe dancer with long black hair, bright red lips and a dress with a long split in the side. She walked up the gangplank of the French boat and whistled loudly.

''Allo boys,' she said in French, ''Ow would you all like to come to a party with lots of pretty girls, silly loaves of bleached white bread a metre long and bowls of hot snails in garlic? There will be an accordion player and second-rate red wine.'[34]

The entire crew of the boat ran towards the Queen, who led them down a very dark alley where Vessel had removed all the manhole covers. In the darkness the Queen and Mordonna helped each sailor make a donation of one pint of blood for baby Valla's breakfasts. The sailors floundered around in the drains for several hours before they realised they weren't at a party. By the time they got back to the harbour, their ship, the *Maldemer*, had vanished.

---

[34] *The French have a reputation, created entirely by the French, for fine food. This includes croissants, which are tiny amounts of pastry holding massive amounts of fat, frogs' legs, snails, and tiny wild birds full of little bones and no meat. And as for accordions, a famous Irish writer once said, 'The only good thing about bagpipes is that they don't smell too.' The same can be said of accordions.*

10

Sail Away

'At last long Snip-Snip got proper crow's nest,' Parsnip said with pride from his new nest at the top of the *Maldemer*'s mast. 'Snip-Snip watch out.'

No one on board had ever been on a boat before. Lake Tarnish is so toxic that any boats on it get eaten away within a few weeks.[35]

'Ahoy land,' Parsnip shouted.

'Thank you, Parsnip,' Vessel called back, 'that's not surprising considering we haven't left the harbour yet.'

---

[35] *Needless to say, the Transylvania Waters Navy is not a career many people choose. Those who do are instantly promoted to the rank of Admiral and awarded a long-service medal two days later.*

'Ahoy harbour,' Parsnip replied.

'Right,' said Vessel, 'we need to find out how to work this thing. I saw a picture of a boat once. I think we're supposed to fix these huge bedsheets to that stick poking up out of the floor.'

'Yes,' the Queen agreed, 'and I think the pointy end should be at the front, not at the back like it is now.'

'What's this thing?' said Nerlin.

'I think it's called a compass,' said the Queen.

'It can't be, there's nowhere to put the pencil to draw a circle with,' said Nerlin.

They hoisted the sails and, as they did, the boat turned itself round and began to sail south-east.

'Which is, er, exactly the direction we want to go,' Vessel lied as he looked at the maps.

Now and then an island or another boat appeared on the horizon, but by pulling on the rudder thing they found hanging over the back of the boat, they managed to keep out of everyone's way.

When the spies reached the harbour, the first people they met were a group of French sailors who smelled as if they had been to a party down a drain.

Cliché asked the sailors if they knew where the spies could get a boat, but the sailors thought they were making fun of the fact they'd lost their own boat, and attacked them. The only good thing about this was that the last bit of the attack involved Cliché, Stain and Ooze being thrown into the harbour, which washed off all the coal dust they had been covered with.

Cliché couldn't swim and neither could Ooze, but as luck would have it the three of them managed to grab hold of a rope hanging down from an old junk.

Seeing this, the French sailors cut the mooring rope and the junk began to drift out of the harbour towards the open sea, with the three spies still

hanging on for dear life and the sailors making rude French hand signals and blowing raspberries.

As she watched the spies clamber up the rope and onto the deck, the Hearse Whisperer realised the junk was about as seaworthy as a paper bag full of marbles. She changed herself into an albatross[36] and flew slowly out to sea.

The junk had not been built for life on the open sea. It had been built to carry bags of very light feathers up and down a very calm river. So it wasn't long before it started leaking.

'Is it supposed to do that?' said Cliché as the water came up round his ankles.

'No, I think the water's supposed to be outside the boat,' said Stain.

'Maybe this is an ancient Chinese submarine,' Ooze suggested.

'If we don't grab those buckets and start bailing out, it'll soon be an ancient Chinese underwater shed,' said Cliché.

They took off all their clothes, tore them into strips and stuffed the strips between the planks. It slowed the water down, but there were too many

---

[36] *An albatross is a huge seabird with an enormous wingspan that can stay at sea for months on end. It is named after the famous Welsh explorer Albert Ross, who also had a shelf in Antarctica and a door handle in Cardiff named after him.*

holes in the junk to stop it completely. All through the day and into the night they took it in turns to empty buckets over the side of the boat.

'I can't lift my arms another inch,' said Ooze, collapsing on the deck. 'If we don't find land soon, we've had it.'

'Is there a map?' said Cliché. 'Let's see if there is any land.'

'Yes, there is a map,' said Stain. 'It's jammed in the big gap in that plank there – and even if we looked at it, what good would it do? It's pitch black, we don't have any instruments, the stars are totally covered by clouds, it's beginning to rain and I want my mummy.'

'Something will turn up,' said Cliché. 'It always does.'

'This time I think the things that are likely to turn up are our toes and a shark,' said Ooze, grabbing Stain. 'I want your mummy too.'

'So do I,' said Cliché, 'and a pair of trousers.'

The boat sank lower and lower in the water as the dark night grew so dark that the three spies

couldn't see their fingers in front of their noses or even find where their noses were. They began to wail and groan in such a pathetic way that it even chased the sharks away.

But, as Cliché had predicted, something did turn up.

It was a bump.

The sinking junk hit something, not with a big crash, but more of a gentle thud that was just hard enough to make the whole boat fall to pieces. Each spy grabbed a plank and hung on. They tried to make their pink legs looks as unappetising as possible by turning blue, just in case the sharks came back.

Night fell and so did the wind, turning the sea to glass. The clouds went off to hassle Belgium and overhead a half moon and a million stars twinkled in an endless sky. Far out of sight of any land, the *Maldemer* sat motionless in the total silence, which was broken only by a whale coughing eighty-four kilometres away.[37]

At last the escapees felt safe. The only sign of life was an albatross circling far above them.

'Ahoy moon,' Parsnip called.

There was a bump and the ship rocked in the water.

'What was that?' said Nerlin.

'What?' said Mordonna.

'That bump. And I can hear voices.'

'Probably just mermaids,' said the Queen. 'You get a lot of them round here.'

---

[37] *There were two more whales coughing, but they were eighty-five kilometres away and therefore out of earshot. It is a well-known scientific fact that you can't hear a whale cough unless it is less than eighty-four kilometres away and only then if the sea is dead calm.*

154

She said this with such confidence that no one thought to ask her how she knew, seeing as how she had never been to sea in her whole life.

'Is that what mermaids do?' Nerlin asked. 'Cry like babies and say they want their mummies?'

'I'm guessing they're probably not mermaids,' said Vessel. 'Get a torch.'

'We haven't got one,' said Mordonna. 'I looked earlier.'

'OK,' said Vessel. He threw some petrol over the side, followed by a match.

The cries of 'I want my mummy' changed into 'I want my mummy and some ointment' and 'Ow, ow, my ear's on fire'.

'Spies ahoy,' said Parsnip.

'Oh, look, it's our three little spies,' said the Queen, 'and they've got surfboards.'

'No, no …' Cliché began.

'Maybe we could whip up some waves for them to ride,' said the Queen. 'I remember having to learn a big wave spell at school. Never could understand why, seeing we didn't have any sea,

but now I suppose it could be useful.'

'No, please, no ...'

'No trouble,' said the Queen. 'Glad to help. I just have to make sure I remember it right, because I think it was right next to the "turning a spy into a jellyfish" spell in the water spells book.'

'No, I, we, err ...' Stain stammered.

The fire had burnt off all his hair except for one tuft so now he looked like an overcooked coconut. The other two looked worse, like burnt coconuts that had been used in a coconut shy at a fun fair.

'Now, don't tell me,' said Vessel. 'There's something you want. That's why you banged our boat.'

'Yes, we –'

Vessel held up his hand. 'No, no, let me guess. Three cold naked spies hanging on to bits of wood, hundreds of miles from land in the middle of the night with a terrible storm approaching ... what on earth could they want?' he said.

'A cup of tea?' said Nerlin.

'Surfboard wax?' said Mordonna.

'Swimming trunks?' said the Queen.

'A towel, that's what it'll be, I bet you,' said Vessel. 'I bet they want a towel.'

'Help,' Cliché bleated in a pathetic voice.

His fingers had gone numb holding onto his plank, and even the plank itself was disappearing as a giant marine woodworm ate it for breakfast.

Vessel threw a rope over the side and hauled the three naked, shivering spies on board. They were each given a sack to wear and then locked in the ship's hold with half a beetroot and a mug of water.

'What are we going to do with them?' asked the Queen.

'Find some remote island that barely supports life and leave them there,' said Vessel. 'Unless you have a better idea.'

'We could keep them as a blood supply for Valla,' Mordonna suggested. 'Fresh food is much healthier for him.'

So each morning Cliché 'donated' a cup of his blood for young Valla's breakfast. Six hours later

Stain 'donated' a cup for Valla's lunch and in the evening Ooze did the same for the boy's dinner.

They spent a few weeks drifting about in the Pacific learning useful sailor-type things, like the fact that one bit of sea looks exactly like another bit of sea and one seagull looks exactly like another seagull, even the girl ones, and young boy wizards do not like seagull blood half as much as spy blood.

'Ahoy ahoy,' shouted Parsnip, getting very excited. 'Snowbits, mountain, place ahoy.'

'Must be South America or Burma,' said Vessel, who had never done geography.

'Ahoy, umm, Snip-Snip look in atlas.'

There was a fluttering of wings from the crow's nest, followed by a lot of sheets of paper blowing away and some swearing.

'Ahoy Chile,' he reported.

'Yes, we are all feeling a bit cold,' said Vessel.

'Not cold skin, got big place Gataponia,' Parsnip explained, which made everything perfectly clear.

Gradually the coast of South America filled the whole horizon. Everyone's spirits began to lift. Weeks of eating the French sailors' food – silly loaves of bleached white bread a metre long and bowls of cold snails in garlic washed down with second-rate red wine – had made them all rather depressed. They were also just about to run out of toilet paper.

As they neared the coast, the sea grew rough. They were at the very bottom of South America, where the seas can be the most ferocious in the world. And they had arrived right in the middle of the rough and stormy season, which would have been hard to avoid since it went from the first of January until the end of December, apart from the odd calm week here and there.

This was not one of those weeks.

Vessel went into the cabin and looked through the ship's library. There was a copy of *How to Sail in Seriously Dangerous Seas for Dummies* but it was all in French. There were also some dictionaries – French/Belgian, Belgian/Serbo–Croat, Serbo–Croat/Cajun and Cajun/English.

'You,' he said, hauling Cliché up into the cabin. 'You've got a French name, what does this book say?'

'Have I?' said Cliché.

'Have you what?'

'Have I got a French name?'

'Yes, Cliché is a French word,' said Vessel.

'What does it mean?'

'I don't know,' said Vessel. 'Hang on, I'll use the dictionaries here. Let's see.'

He flicked through the pages, translating language after language, and finally said, 'Cliché in English translates as ... umm, cliché.'

'Oh, thanks for clearing that up.'

Since it had taken five minutes to go through the four dictionaries to find out Cliché meant cliché, by the time Vessel had translated a single sentence, they would have smashed into the dangerous rocks that were now on all sides of them.

'Here, give it to me,' said the Queen, doing the French cafe dancer trick again to make sure they would obey.

161

Vessel and Cliché both fainted. When they came round, Vessel locked Cliché back in the hold and slapped him for fainting at the Queen's beauty, which only Vessel was allowed to do.

'It says, *ma cherie*,' the Queen said, turning the pages of the book, 'zat unless you are a sailor extraordinaire *avec le* tons of experience, you should keep away from ze rocks *avec* ze sharp pointy bits.'

'I think we kind of knew that already,' said Nerlin.

'*Exactement*,' said the Queen. 'It ees a stupid *livre*.'

There was a list of correct sailing terms in the back of the book, which only confused them even more. Apparently the ropes that were tied to the sheets were called sheets. The things they had called sheets were called sails and the pointy end of the boat was called the front.

'So what are the white cotton things we put on our beds then?' Mordonna asked.

'It doesn't say,' said the Queen, 'but seeing as

how the ropes are the sheets I imagine the sheets would be the ropes.'

'The sooner we get to dry land, the better,' Nerlin muttered.

11
Stormy Seas

The Hearse Whisperer had landed on top of Cape Horn and changed back into the closest thing to a human she could manage. As she stood looking down into the angry sea, the *Maldemer* sailed into view. Tierra del Fuego was not called the land of fire for nothing and it didn't take much effort on the secret, secret agent's part to whip the storm up into an almighty frenzy.

Two hundred and seventeen penguins huddled together on the rocks at the foot of the cliffs waiting for the storm to pass. The Hearse Whisperer lifted the birds into the air and dropped them onto the *Maldemer*. They waved their sad little wings and

stuck their feet out in front of them in a feeble attempt to fly, but instead they fell into the already fragile sails, tearing them to shreds, before they landed in a wet, miserable, confused pile on the deck. The violent wind ripped the tattered sails from the mast and carried them away. With each giant wave, the poor penguins ran from one side of the boat to the other. Instead of sinking it as the Hearse Whisperer had hoped, they helped to keep it upright.

One penguin missed the deck and got stuck in the top of the narrow funnel that ran up from the engine, which Vessel and Nerlin had built out of

the rest of the chopsticks, an enormous jellyfish and four of Mordonna's toenail clippings,[38] bringing the ship to a sudden stop. No matter how hard Nerlin pulled on the rope, the engine refused to restart.

'Right, you three,' said Vessel, hauling Cliché, Stain and Ooze up from the hold, 'up on deck, you have to man the oars.'

The three spies complained and begged and promised that if they ever got safely home again they would devote the rest of their lives to helping little old ladies cross the street, even little old ladies who didn't know they wanted to cross, but Vessel and Nerlin poked and pushed them up onto the deck.

'Start rowing,' said Vessel.

'Aren't you guys going to row as well?' Ooze whimpered.

'There are only three sets of oars,' said Nerlin, 'and besides, I've got to steer the ship and Vessel's got to do the washing up.'

---

[38] *Don't try this at home. It only works if you are a wizard, otherwise you just end up with a sticky mess.*

166

'Vet, vet, vet, Snip-Snip got vet on head,' said Parsnip. 'Vith the tovel make Snip-Snip dry as.'

After three minutes pulling the oars with all their might, the three spies collapsed from exhaustion. The ship had moved three-point-six centimetres eastwards.

'Faster!' Vessel demanded.

'We can't,' said Cliché.

'We're done for,' cried Stain.

'We're all going to die,' sobbed Ooze.

'You're forgetting something,' said Vessel. 'Five of us are wizards. Wizards do not drown at sea. Wizards can only be drowned in the Terrible Pool of Vestor and that is thousands of miles from here.'

'We're not wizards,' Cliché cried.

'True,' said Vessel. 'You three could very well be going to die.'

'That,' said Nerlin, untangling a penguin from his hair, 'is why you need to row faster. The faster you row, the faster we get out of here into the Atlantic.'

'Boat sink, then Snip-Snip do Albert Ross and sore on vind,' said Parsnip. 'Snip-Snip safe bee.'

The storm increased in ferocity. It made no difference how hard the three spies pulled on their oars. They were drifting slowly backwards out of control towards the sharpest pointy rock in the whole area. The sea was so wild that rowing was

like trying to stir sugar into a fifty-metre-wide cup of tea with a very, very tiny twig. If there had been a hundred people rowing, it would have made no difference, except, of course, that if there *had* been a hundred people on the *Maldemer*, it would have sunk because it was a small boat.

The waves began lifting rocks right up from the ocean floor and the first thing the rocks did was smash the ends off the six oars the spies were rowing with.

'That's better,' said Stain, pulling his sticks backwards. 'I seem to have found a new strength.'

'Me too,' said Cliché and Ooze in unison.

The Hearse Whisperer summoned massive heavy clouds that turned the day to night and dropped raindrops as big as footballs. Nerlin ran round the deck picking up stunned penguins and passing them down to Mordonna in the cabin below, where the soggy birds waddled around drinking all the water that was coming
into the boat.

It is often said that every cloud has a silver lining, but no one ever says that some of them have a vulture lining too.

Mordonna's faithful old bird, Leach, who had been slowly making his way towards Patagonia, had been swept up high into the air by an angry trade wind as he had crossed the equator. It had carried him right into a bank of rain clouds that were so far above the world that he could hardly get enough oxygen to breathe. He had tried to fly down or even fall down, but the clouds had kept him imprisoned in their thick folds. Fortunately the clouds were on their way to South America, having been summoned there by the Hearse Whisperer to join in the storm, and as they dumped all their rain over land and sea, they dropped Leach into a clump of stunted bushes on the mountain above the Hearse Whisperer.

Leach had limited powers, nothing like those of a true witch or wizard, but he had enough to screech at the sky until it began to calm down.

The Hearse Whisperer spun round to find

whoever was calming her storm but, squashed between scrubby bushes, Leach was too well hidden.

No matter, thought the Hearse Whisperer. *We will move on. Time to leave this godforsaken place.*

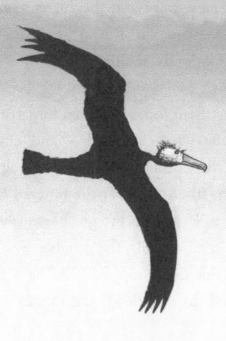

Tristan da Cunha

12

The sea grew calm and the current carried the *Maldemer* out into the vast emptiness of the Atlantic Ocean. By taking all the sheets off the beds – which took some organising because they kept calling them ropes and then forgetting they'd swapped the names around – and cutting up everyone's spare undies, Mordonna and the Queen managed to stitch together the tattered remnants of the old sails that hadn't got blown overboard, and make a small sail. The trouble was that the wind had not only stopped blowing a storm, it had gone off for a lie-down and the sea was as flat as glass.

'Where are we going?' Nerlin asked as they drifted helplessly on the ocean current.

'Well, according to my compass,' said Vessel, taking out his geometry set and drawing a circle with a pencil and compass on a sheet of paper, 'we are heading in a sort of northerly direction, give or take three hundred and sixty degrees.'

'OK,' said Mordonna, 'so where is the nearest land?'

'Umm, err, there isn't any,' said Vessel. 'Though I think I can say with some confidence we are probably going to a country that begins with "A".'

'Snip-Snip wery pleased not country with a wubble you or a wee,' said Parsnip.

'Yes,' Vessel continued. 'I'm pretty sure we are headed for Africa. Or America.'

'Not Austria then?' said Nerlin, who had a terrible sense of direction and hadn't even heard of the word geography.

'Well, this is just brilliant,' snapped Mordonna, slapping the three spies, who were slumped over their broken oars, with a wet fish. 'You do know

173

I'm going to have another baby quite soon, don't you?'

No one did, though they could see why it might make her annoyed enough to slap people with a wet fish.

The Atlantic Ocean is seriously big. You could sail for days and days all over it, or even months if you kept getting your ropes and bed clothes tangled up with your sheets. You would see nothing except water, bits of dead seaweed, bits of alive seaweed, discarded burger boxes, lost thongs, fourteen albatrosses and more water that looked exactly the same as the first bit of water.

However, right in the middle of this cosmically huge desert of wet nothing, there is one tiny island. It is the tip of a huge underwater volcano, and it's called Tristan da Cunha. It is such a tiny and remote place that it wasn't even on the map that Vessel was using – and he had one of the best maps that had ever been given away as a free insert in *The Junior Wizard's Fun Weekly* comic.[39] So when it appeared on the horizon directly ahead of them, they thought it was Africa.

'Isn't that amazing?' said the Queen. 'I always thought Africa was bigger than that.'

'Maybe it's a lot further away,' said Nerlin.

'Go see,' said Vessel, and Parsnip flew off, circled the tiny island, all thirty-eight square miles of it, and was back five minutes later.

'Africa shrunk done,' he said. 'And ahoy no pymarids, all stolen.'

'Maybe it's Atlantis,' Nerlin suggested.

---

[39] *Published every thirteen days by Haphazard Quarters at 17 Dripping Goat Lane, Big Town, Transylvania Waters. Annual subscription – three gold sovereigns plus one litre of blood.*

'Ahoy not Atlantis, big bang come say hello,' Parsnip called down from his crow's nest. A second later the *Maldemer* came to a sudden halt due to the fact that it had hit Tristan da Cunha, proving that it *is* possible to find a needle in a haystack.

Fifteen sheep wandered down from a field and looked at them.

'Ah,' said the Queen, 'it's the welcoming committee.'

The fifteen sheep were followed by a man and a dog.

'Have you got permission to land?' said the man.

'Permission?' said Vessel. 'We are shipwrecked mariners in dire need of assistance.'

'Fair enough,' said the man. 'Have a potato.'

'Wonderful,' said the Queen. 'What we actually need is hot water and towels. My daughter is about to have a baby.'

'What's a towel?' said the man. 'Could you use a potato instead? We've got lots of them. Or a prawn? We've billions of them.'

After a few more minutes of this weird conversation, the man led them up the beach to a place called Potato Patches, where there was a small hut. While the man wasn't looking, the Queen cast a spell over a pile of potatoes, turning them into a comfy bed, several hot towels and a heated bottle of French mineral water with a dash of lime. At least, that was what she had intended to turn them into. What she ended up with was an armchair covered

in the tartan of the McSnaughty clan, three tea towels showing detailed maps of Tristan da Cunha *before* the new hut had been built, bordered with a frieze of potatoes, and a bottle of Belgian beetroot-flavoured mineral water. Her wand wasn't working properly because the strange man had turned it into a seafood kebab by sticking six prawns and a potato ring on it.

'Damn wand,' she said, bashing it against the doorframe to shake off the food.

As Mordonna's second child, Satanella, was born, the Queen hit her wand a second time. There was a flash of lightning. The air was filled with the smell of fried prawns and the tiny, perfectly formed little baby, lying in Mordonna's adoring arms, was turned into a small black puppy with pointy teeth. Before the Queen could reverse the spell, the wand turned to dust and vanished in the wind.

'Oops,' she said.

'Snip-Snip love puppy wery cuddling,' said Parsnip. 'Big hugs, wery, wery good luck blessing.'

'Shut up, Parsnip,' said Vessel.

The sheep farmer poked his head round the door and, pointing at Satanella, said that his own dog was getting too old to round up the sheep and he'd be happy to give them sixty-five potatoes for the puppy.

'I'm not a puppy, you stupid man,' said Satanella, who hadn't actually seen herself in a mirror yet. 'I'm a baby girl.'

The man fainted. What Satanella said when

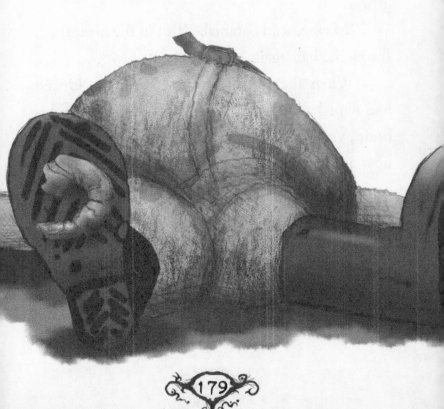

she looked down at her paws is too rude to repeat, but after a chew on a lamb bone, a bit of a run between the potato plants chasing a red rubber ball, and a lick of a few bits of her body that humans and even witches shouldn't be able to reach, she decided that life as a dog might not be that bad.

'When we get out of here and settle down into a place of our own,' Mordonna said, 'Granny will get a new wand and turn you back into a little girl.'

'Maybe,' said Satanella. 'But in the meantime, throw the ball again.'

When the islander came to and the Queen had wiped all memory of a talking puppy from his brain, Vessel brought the three spies ashore from the boat and the islander took them all along the track to Edinburgh, the largest settlement on the island. Being the only settlement on the island it was also the smallest settlement, the nicest settlement, the settlement with the best potatoes and the settlement most likely to get traffic lights if the island ever got any roads or traffic.

'We've applied for a traffic light grant from London, just in case,' said the man.

The three spies were an instant hit with Tristan da Cunha's young women. There was a lack of eligible young men on the island and the sight of these three new men made the girls giggle and blush with excitement.

'Nice sack,' said the boldest girl, sidling up to Cliché and stroking the coarse hessian.

The three spies couldn't believe their luck. Back in Transylvania Waters they were always the ones left on their own at dances and their most popular nickname among the Transylvanian Waters girls was 'loser'. But now they had their choice of seventeen adoring fans.

The Hearse Whisperer, now in the form of a giant sea eagle, sat on the very top of Tristan da Cunha and watched everything. She was very pleased when the islander invited the three useless spies to stay on Tristan da Cunha. She could have simply turned Cliché, Stain and Ooze into lobsters, but she thought that maybe one day in the future

she might want them for something, and this tiny isolated island was the perfect place to store them. No matter how miserable their lives became, they would never be able to leave.

After a brief negotiation, which involved six potatoes and a lobster changing hands, it was agreed that Cliché, Stain and Ooze would give up spying and stay on Tristan da Cunha. There would be a lottery and the three winning ticket holders would each get an ex-spy as a husband. The three happy couples would get one week's honeymoon in a hut on Inaccessible Island and the runners-up

would each get a potato carved in the shape of a husband and a place at the top of the queue when the next boat with any spies on arrived.

The island had recently had a population increase of four, when some rams had been sent over four thousand kilometres from the Falkland Islands to increase the mutton gene pool. Now the three ex-spies would do the same for the human gene pool.

After a hearty meal of potatoes and prawns, washed down with lashings of potato and prawn wine, the visitors were given a souvenir potato each, personally autographed by the island council, and shown to their beds, where they slept like logs.[40]

Just after dawn, while the population of two hundred and seventy-four[41] was still fast asleep,

---

[40] *Except they didn't get attacked by wood-borers like logs often do.*

[41] *Visit http://www.tristandc.com to find out more wonderful facts about Tristan da Cunha, including the annual ratting day, when a prize is given for the longest rat tail of the day. You can even join the Tristan da Cunha Association. I know I have. You will also discover that there really is a place there called 'Potato Patches'.*

Vessel shook everyone awake and led them quietly back to the *Maldemer*.

'We'll leave them a present to thank them for their hospitality,' he whispered as they left the village. Waving his wand, he conjured up a set of bright new traffic lights right in the middle of the village. Unfortunately, Vessel was not very scientifically minded and forgot to leave any controls for the lights, so they were permanently set on red. This caused a lot of problems in the village until someone made a new footpath so everyone could walk around the lights without breaking the law.

'Next stop, err, somewhere beginning with "A",' said Vessel.

'America,' said Satanella. 'I want America.'

'I want Africa,' said Valla.

'What about Argentina?' Nerlin suggested. 'Or Australia.'

'Or Amsterdam?' said Mordonna.

'Or anywhere?' said the Queen.

'Auntie Noreen's,' said Parsnip.

184

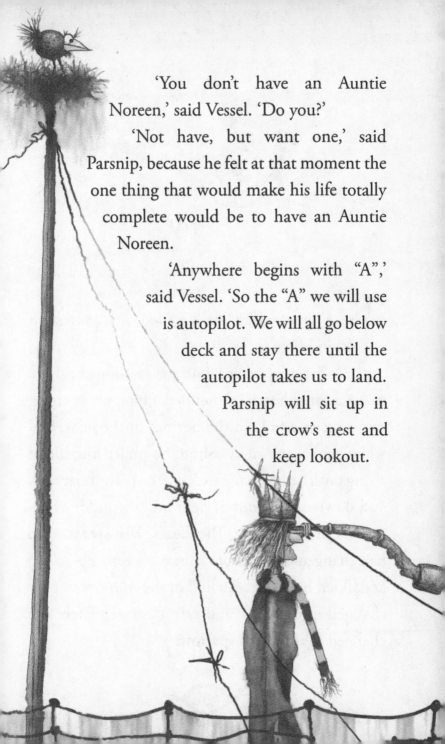

'You don't have an Auntie Noreen,' said Vessel. 'Do you?'

'Not have, but want one,' said Parsnip, because he felt at that moment the one thing that would make his life totally complete would be to have an Auntie Noreen.

'Anywhere begins with "A",' said Vessel. 'So the "A" we will use is autopilot. We will all go below deck and stay there until the autopilot takes us to land. Parsnip will sit up in the crow's nest and keep lookout.

13

The 'A' where they finally ended their journey is shrouded in secrecy.

Under cover of darkness they slipped ashore on a deserted beach. Vessel tied a long bit of string to a cork in a hole in the bottom of the boat, and when they were safely ashore he pulled the bit of string until he heard the cork pop out. The boat sank and slowly settled out of sight into the mud, where it remains to this day. The Hearse Whisperer, who had changed herself from a sea eagle into a barnacle and glued herself to the hull of the *Maldemer*, now changed into a duck and swam ashore, where she changed again into a sparrow.

'We need to find an estate agent,' said the Queen.

'Haven't we been through enough horrible stuff already?' said Mordonna.

'Our best way to stay hidden from the King's spies is to find a remote house in a big forest as far as possible from any other houses,' said the Queen.

'I don't agree, my dear,' said Vessel. 'Remote houses miles from anywhere will be the first place they'll look.'

'Even if it is,' said the Queen, 'it would take them years to find us.'

'I have a better idea,' said Vessel. 'The best place to hide is the last place they would look and that is right in the middle of a human city in an ordinary house in an ordinary street.'

So, in extremely heavy disguises that made them look as human as most people in seaside bed and breakfasts in winter do, Nerlin, Mordonna, the two children and the Queen booked into Seagull View, a grey, nondescript hotel three streets back from the sea front. Here they had to suffer far

worse things than they had ever had to whilst at sea. They had to eat salty porridge for breakfast, share a bathroom with a Morris-Dancing group who kept practising all night for the upcoming World Silly Dancing Olympics, and they were forced to sleep in rooms with dreadful wallpaper covered in suspicious stains.

Meanwhile, Vessel went in search of their new home. Although he thought they would be safer in a normal house in the middle of the city, he agreed to look for a big old house miles and miles from anywhere because he was totally in love with the Queen. He changed into a crow and flew with Parsnip out into the countryside.

The Hearse Whisperer flew behind them.

The seaside town gave way to fields and small villages.

'Too many people there,' Vessel said and the two of them flew on.

The fields gave way to open country and a large forest that stretched away to the horizon.

'This looks promising,' said Vessel, landing on the top branch of a tall tree.

Here and there dirt tracks cut wavy lines through the trees, but they all seemed to lead to dead ends. Vessel and Parsnip split up and flew down different tracks, returning to the tall tree every hour. Below them, hiding under a big leaf, the Hearse Whisperer had collapsed, exhausted.

Sparrows have much smaller wings than crows and she had had a terrible time keeping up with Vessel and Parsnip. Given a choice, she would have changed herself into an eagle, but form-changing wasn't something you could do too often without bursting lots of veins inside your head and turning into a second-hand car salesman for ever and ever.

It was dusk before Vessel finally found a house. From the air, it looked perfect: semi-derelict but watertight, overgrown with deadly nightshade and ivy, home to a family of bats and armies of spiders. What more could a family of wizards ask for? Perhaps the Queen had been right. Perhaps this *was* the perfect place for the Floods to settle down. It was certainly far more appealing than any house in suburbia could be.

He flew back to the tree to tell Parsnip.

'We'll go and spend the night there,' Vessel said. 'You can only get the true feel for a place in the dangerous hours after midnight. There may be ghosts and we'll need to make sure they're friendly.'

As midnight struck, something made the hairs in his throat tingle and Vessel knew there was danger nearby. He tried to ignore it, but it was like when you know you are going to be sick – no matter how still you keep and how much you try to sleep in the hope it will go away, you know that it will never go away until you have thrown up. Whatever you do is just putting it off until later.

Vessel tried to think nice thoughts, like himself and the Queen sitting hand in hand in a big hammock on the veranda watching the moon and listening to the owls tearing tiny mice to pieces in the moonlight. It was the most perfect daydream he had ever had and, since the Queen had shown that she cared for him as much as he cared for her, he had realised that the dream could actually become real. Yet it still seemed too good to be true.

And when something seems too good to be true, he thought, *it usually is.*

There was someone else in the room. Vessel knew he should have changed back from being a crow, but now, as he began the spell, the someone

191

grabbed him round the neck, stuffed him into an enchanted birdcage and sprayed him with SuperStickIt, which meant he would stay in the form he was until he was rinsed off in the Terrible Pool of Vestor.

'Change back now if you can,' said the someone.

'Hearse Whisperer?' said Vessel.

'Yes. You might have been clever enough to thwart Cliché, Stain and Ooze,' said the Hearse Whisperer, back in her real form, 'but you can't fool me.'

'Can we talk about this?' said Vessel, playing for time to let Parsnip slip off into the night before the Hearse Whisperer saw him.

If his assistant could reach the Queen before the Hearse Whisperer – and if the Queen could actually understand what the crow was saying – the runaways would be able to escape and disappear into the heart of some big city.

'What's to talk about?' said the Hearse Whisperer.

'We could work together,' said Vessel. 'The Queen is the only one I care about, not the others. If I helped you and you agreed not to harm the Queen, we could easily kidnap Mordonna and take her back to the King.'

'Umm, maybe,' said the Hearse Whisperer, suspiciously. 'I'm not sure I can trust you. I'll sleep on it.'

She hung Vessel's cage up on a hook and lay down on the floor to sleep.

Trapped in the enchanted cage, Vessel was powerless, but at least he had bought a good six hours' time. He nibbled the cuttlefish stuck between the bars and fell into a deep depression.

He had failed his one true love. Even if the Hearse Whisperer fell for his trick and she did take Mordonna back to the King, the Queen would never forgive Vessel for any part he might have had in the plot. Also, he couldn't stand the taste of cuttlefish. It tasted like something that had come out of the inside of a squid.

'Will you stop with the wretched cuttlefish?' the Hearse Whisperer snapped. 'I'm trying to sleep.'

Meanwhile, Parsnip had reached the B&B and sat on the windowsill tapping feebly at the glass. Nerlin opened the window and lifted the soggy, exhausted bird inside.

'Are you Vessel or Parsnip?' said the Queen.

'Snip-Snip,' said Parsnip. 'Wessel lost, gone bye bye.'

'Not dead?' cried the Queen. 'Not my beloved Vessel, my one true love, cut off in his prime at a mere hundred and twenty years of age, a star that shone so brightly in this sad world of ours, now turned into a black hole lost in the mists of time, my genius and protector gone from my life forever, leaving us all alone and desolate to fend for ourselves and our children and our children's children without his magic, his mystery, his dark sombre voice and his exceptionally well-fitting tights?'

'No.'

'What?'

'Wessel not dead, him twapped in urnchanted cagey wire thing by worse hisperer,' said Parsnip.

'Oh no,' cried the Queen.

'Right,' said Mordonna, taking charge. 'We must get out of here immediately. With a bit of luck we've got a few hours' start and should be able to get away.'

'I will stay,' said the Queen, 'in case my true love, my only ...'

'No you won't. You'll do as you're told and come with us,' Mordonna ordered. 'I'm going to have another baby fairly soon, you know, so I'd like to get settled into somewhere safe. We can look for Vessel later.'

So they took a cab to the station, a train to another city, another cab to a different station, another train to a third city, walked across the road, got on a bus to yet another station, and

went to a fourth city that was not so much a city as a large town.

Just to make doubly sure they would not be followed, they covered their tracks with garlic powder then walked backwards to another station where they took the fifteenth train to a town that was so ugly no one would ever think they would choose to live there, even if they were playing a double-triple-quadruple-bluff. Then they bought a street map.

'Right, let's have a look,' said Mordonna, unfolding the map. 'We need a nice anonymous street ... Wow, I don't believe it.'

'What?'

'Which plant scares wizards more than any other?'

'Deadly nightshade?' said Nerlin.

'No, that's their favourite. Which one is the opposite?'

'White roses?'

'Worse.'

'Not the "A" plant?'

198

'Exactly. Acacias,' said Mordonna, crossing her fingers for protection.[42] 'You'll never believe this but there's a street in this town called Acacia Avenue.'

'See, I told you humans were stupid,' said the Queen.

'Yes, we all know that,' said Mordonna, 'but if we bought a house in Acacia Avenue, it would be the last place the King's spies would ever look for us.'

'But wouldn't we all burst out in huge warty boils and die horribly if we went to live there?' said Nerlin.

'Of course not,' said Mordonna, pretending to be brave. 'That's just an old wives tale.'

'I'm an old wife,' said the Queen. 'And I believe it.'

But Mordonna insisted, and to prove it was all silly superstition she made Parsnip fly down Acacia

---

[42] *The reason wizards and witches are terrified of Acacias is so secret that even I don't know it, and if I do ever find out, I won't be able to tell you because if I do I'll have to kill you.*

Avenue and back. Then she walked down the street herself and then she walked down it again taking her two children with her. Finally, she made Nerlin and the Queen walk down it.

'And,' she said, when the others had reluctantly agreed she might be right, 'did you notice that there was a For Sale sign on one of the houses?'

'No,' said Nerlin, the Queen, Valla and Satanella all at once. 'I had my eyes shut.'

'And how's this for a good omen?' Mordonna went on. 'It's the luckiest number in the world, number thirteen.'

So they drew straws and the loser went and got the estate agent. The Queen paid for the house with the King's gold, and they moved in to their new home.

Dry Land 14

'I t would be good if we could get all the furniture sorted out first,' said Mordonna to Nerlin as they walked through the empty house, 'because I'd like to have another baby very soon.'

As the whole family were witches and wizards, they didn't have to bother with all the usual shopping stuff.[43] All they had to do was concentrate on what they wanted and do a few spells with Mordonna's wand.

The Queen, who was reduced to using her

---

[43] *Like getting the bus down to the shops and window shopping and having to talk to salesmen in cheap suits trying to pretend their solid oak furniture was not actually made out of recycled cardboard.*

second-best wand since the accident in Tristan da Cunha, was still too upset at losing Vessel to concentrate. After she filled the lounge room with crocodiles instead of comfy chairs, she was only allowed to get smaller household items like the kettle and toothbrushes.[44]

Remembering what the Sheman had said about having seven children, Nerlin was given the job of

[44] *Not quite sure why the Queen got toothbrushes because all witches and wizards have a very small vampire beetle that cleans their teeth while they are asleep — see the back of this book for more information.*

adding more space to the house.

So as not to arouse suspicion with the neighbours when a whole lot of new rooms suddenly appeared, he hid three rooms in the attic and created some more underground, including lots of cellars where each member of the family could enjoy their own special hobbies or experiments to their heart's content. It was only when he had dug down so far that he could fry an egg on the floor using the heat at the centre of the earth that he decided it was time to stop.

About five minutes after the Floods finished

furnishing the house, the most incredible thunderstorm started. At first they thought the Hearse Whisperer had somehow managed to track them down, but it was just a coincidence.

Parsnip had always been a big fan of thunderstorms, especially lightning, so he decided to fly up to the tallest chimney and become a lightning conductor.

'Ven Wessel back is, me be bird again,' he said and flew out into the rain to conduct the storm.

By the time Mordonna was ready to have her third baby, Parsnip had reached the fifth movement of his storm symphony and the thunder was exploding wonderfully through the black clouds. The crow raised his baton and massive bolts of lightning raced round and round number thirteen Acacia Avenue. Enough electricity to power the whole of New York for seventeen months shot through the bedroom window at the very moment the baby was born.

And in that instant all the lightning vanished.

And Mordonna got a huge shock.

Actually she got two huge shocks, and they were both from the baby. The first one was a huge electric shock and the second was a huge shock to her eyes. The baby was covered from head to foot in wiry hair. Even the palms of its hands and in between its toes were hairy and every hair was crackling with the lightning it had absorbed. In the darkness caused by a power cut, the baby's eyes sparkled like two light bulbs.

'All that lightning,' said the Queen. 'Is it dead?'

'Far from it,' said Mordonna. 'It's got a huge grin on its face.'

While the baby touched the brass bed with its fingers, making it glow and hover around the room, the Queen brought Mordonna a pair of heavy lead gloves so she could hold her new baby.

'If it's a girl, let's call it Mary,' she said dreamily.

'If it's a boy, we should name it after my most famous ancestor, Merlin,' Nerlin said.

They both peered closely at the baby, but couldn't find any clues to what it was. All their attempts to find out ended up with everyone getting an electric shock, even when they used a pair of rubber gloves and some barbecue tongs. In the end they decided that it didn't really matter.

'Well, Merlinmary it is,' Mordonna said brightly. 'I wonder what you feed an electric baby.'

'Bat trees, bat trees,' Merlinmary said. 'Me want bat trees.'

So they brought her bats but she just electrocuted them. They tried her with blood and everything else they had in the kitchen, but Merlinmary didn't like any of them.

'If I remember rightly,' said the Queen, 'I had a distant cousin three times removed – Binky Frankenstein – and she had the same problem. I think they fed her batteries.'

'Bat trees!' Merlinmary repeated.

She stuck her fingers in the electric socket[45]

---

[45] *Not only must you NEVER try this at home, you must NEVER try it anywhere else either.*

and all the lights in Acacia Avenue went out.

'Maybe you should just use one finger next time,' Mordonna suggested.

Despite the late-night happy sounds of Valla sucking blood, Satanella yapping and Merlinmary buzzing quietly, the Queen couldn't settle down. She spent all night every night pacing up and down on the back verandah. If *you* did this for several nights, you would look dreadful. With the Queen it was difficult to see any difference.

'Mother, you look like death warmed up,' Mordonna said. 'Actually, no, you always look like that. Now you look like death gone cold. But you shouldn't give up hope. I'm sure you'll see Vessel again.'

'That's easy for you to say, but together we're hundreds of years old already! How long do you

suggest I wait before giving up hope?'

'Maybe we could send Parsnip to look for him,' Nerlin suggested.

'If we do that it could alert the Hearse Whisperer to where we are,' said the Queen. 'No, I've made a decision. I want to be buried in the back garden. If my sweetheart ever comes back, you can dig me up again.'

If you are a witch and you get buried in a coffin, it doesn't necessarily mean you're dead. It just means you've decided to stop being alive for a while, which is not the same thing. So Nerlin went down into his cellar and made the old lady a comfy coffin with a TV and an internit connection[46] and a funnel for rat-tail soup – a special recipe from Tristan Da Cunha. Because she was one of those frantic little dogs that loves to dig, Satanella spent the next three days making a huge hole in the back garden.

When it was ready, Nerlin lowered the coffin

---

[46] *Sort of like an internet connection, but instead of messages being carried by phone lines and satellites, they are carried down little tunnels by nits on the back of trained millipedes.*

into place. The Queen put on a clean shroud, got a copy of the latest TV guide and a nice embroidered cushion saying 'Death Is Not A Rehearsal', and climbed in.

Nerlin screwed down the lid, connected the TV to the power and plugged in the soup funnel. Then Satanella scraped all the earth back over the

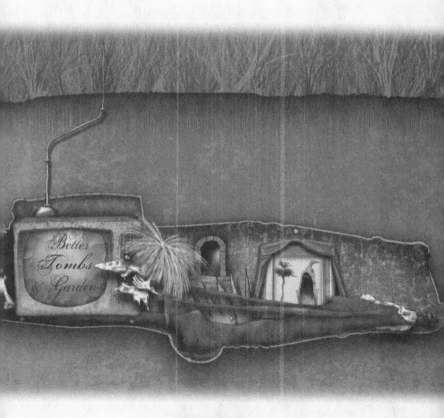

coffin. Mordonna patted it down with a spade and planted a nice group of funeral lilies round the edge.

The Queen admitted to herself that she was too old to go gallivanting around any more and that long afternoons in the airless gloom of a comfy coffin watching old black and white movies on TV and being slowly eaten away by maggots would actually be rather nice.

'If you hear anything about my beloved Vessel,' she shouted through the funnel, 'just send me a fleamail over the nit.'

Over the next few weeks the Floods

settled in to their new home. The Hearse Whisperer searched backwards and forwards, up and down, sideways and in a wiggly spiral trying to find the family, but with no luck. Rather than admit they had eluded her, she convinced herself that they had left the country, so she left the country too. If only the Floods had known this, they could have sent Parsnip off to find Vessel and bring him back.

Leach, being a homing vulture, had no trouble finding them – although he had almost been persuaded to stay in Patagonia by a very attractive condor that had fluttered her throat at him and fed him dainty morsels of festering meat. The Flood family thought the sight of a huge ugly old bird flapping around Acacia Avenue might be too much for the locals, though, so Leach agreed to go and look for Vessel.

'It's either that, or I could turn you into a budgie,' telepathed Mordonna.

'Tough choice,' Leach telepathed back. 'Fly through endless rain and storms and blizzards into the unknown or become a cute little blue thing sitting in a cage eating disgusting cuttlefish and asking everyone who's a pretty boy then. I'll see you later.'

And he flew off in the totally wrong direction, which would probably become the right direction – eventually.

'You know, Nerlin, my darling,' Mordonna said as they watched their three children racing

around the house, 'the Sheman may have said seven children, but after one of the last two being turned into a dog because a prawn was in the wrong place at the wrong time, and the other being struck by lightning, I think we might make the other four with a book of spells and a selection of common household ingredients.'

THE GLAND That Time FORGOT

POINTED STICKS

DRAGON'S MILK

DARK FLUIDS

DANGEROUS DOUBLE STRENGTH

13 Acacia Avenue

Winchflat Flood mostly created himself. Mordonna bought a packet of freeze-dried wizpoles[47] by mail-order from Transylvania Waters, being careful to use a false name on the order form. Nerlin took one wizpole down into the cellars and put it into a tank of special hatching brew, which he made from an ancient recipe his grandmother had tattooed on the underneath of his tongue.

What should have happened then is that the wizpole should have slowly grown into a baby wizard by growing arms and legs and learning to

---

[47] *The wizard version of a tadpole.*

breathe air. What actually happened was that Nerlin dropped a minute scrap of bacon from a sandwich he'd been eating into the tank and it joined with the wizpole and slowly began to mutate.

Time passed and, as it did so, a tiny innocent worm tunnelled down from the back garden until it fell through a gap in the cellar roof and landed in the tank. By then Winchflat had grown his arms and legs and he swam over to the worm and swallowed it. At that very moment the brightest full moon of the century rose over Acacia Avenue and sent a tiny beam of light right down the tunnel the worm had made. As the light moved towards the cellar, it was magnified by minute specks of quartz in the earth, so that when it burst into the cellar it was as strong as a five-megawatt laser. It hit Winchflat right on the back of the head and transferred all its power into his brain.

I think, therefore I am, Winchflat thought and immediately grew eyes, a nose, giant ears and extra fingers and toes.

I am a ladder, he thought, *the Lord of the*

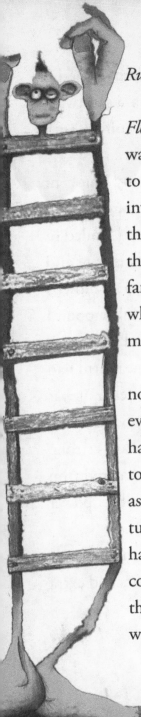

Rungs, and he climbed out of the tank.

Finally he thought, *I am Winchflat Flood, the Lord of the Things,* which was right, because Winchflat was to be the family genius who would invent and build many wonderful things such as the Solid Photocopier that could clone living beings, and the fantastic Seethebackofyourheadascope, which one day would turn him into a multi-millionaire.

But Winchflat's genius alone was not enough. Without the final incredible event in the series of coincidences that had created him, he would have starved to death, because tiny babies, even ones as incredibly brilliant as Winchflat turned out to be, cannot reach door handles. By a mega-double-incredible coincidence, Mordonna went down to that particular cellar to store a piece of washed-rind cheese that was so smelly

216

that even when it was buried in concrete inside a steel safe, it made your eyes water for a week.

'I thought I was going to have another baby,' she said when she saw her newly created son. 'Who's a clever boy then?'

'I am, Mummy,' said Winchflat. He proceeded to recite his eighteen times table in seven hundred languages, none of which was Belgian.[48]

'Well, four down, three to go,' said Nerlin when Mordonna arrived in the kitchen with their new baby.

'I was thinking,' said Mordonna, 'maybe we could have twins or even triplets and get the whole seven-baby prediction out of the way in one go.'

So baby Winchflat designed his first invention, using assorted plastic bottles, PVC pipes from the building site down the road, six toilet roll tubes, an experimental nuclear power plant, some chemicals, a set of Jamie Oliver saucepans and a dash of Worcestershire Sauce. They tried to construct the

---

[48] *Which just goes to show how smart he was.*

machine in the cellar where Winchflat had been created, but the washed-rind cheese had mutated into a chartered accountant who wouldn't let them into the room because he still smelled like old mouldy socks and was very embarrassed.

'Hold on,' said Winchflat. 'If you want twins we need one more thing.'

'What's that, my darling boy?' said Mordonna.

'A mirror.'

So, in the end, the machine was built in the porcelain sink in the upstairs bathroom, underneath the vanity mirror. Winchflat put the finishing touches to his invention, then Nerlin lit the blue touchpaper and ran away.

There was a quiet explosion and when the smoke had cleared the sink was no longer full of toilet rolls and miscellaneous objects but was overflowing with twin baby boys. The two boys looked at each other and gurgled, one morbidly, the other silently. Mordonna and Nerlin knew exactly what to call them.

Later the whole family sat on the back

verandah, drinking warm blood slurpies as the ice-cold moon rose over the trees and illuminated the funeral lilies on Queen Scratchrot's grave.

'One more,' said Mordonna.

'Another slurpie, dearest?' said Nerlin.

'No, darling. One more baby,' said Mordonna. 'A nice sweet little girl.'

'Just because the Sheman said we would have seven children doesn't mean we have to,' said Nerlin. 'Everyone knows that Shemans are rubbish at numbers.'

'That could mean we have fifteen children,' said Mordonna.

Nerlin went as white as the funeral lilies. The

Nerlin is here, but he's turned SO white you can't see him.

219

colour even drained away from his blood slurpie. He was quiet for a while.

'I suppose one more wouldn't hurt,' he said finally. 'After all, we seem to have given your father's agents the slip. It's safe here.'

'Exactly,' said Mordonna. 'I want a pretty little girl and not one made in a jam jar or a cellar.'

'OK, my darling.'

'I think that then,' said Mordonna, 'life would probably be perfect.'

EPILOGUE [49]

Back in Transylvania Waters, Prince Nochyn of Battenberg and his entire family of sixty-three relations had arrived for the Prince's grand wedding to Princess Mordonna.

The King tried to stall them in the hope that the Hearse Whisperer would bring her back, but after six months, he had to admit the truth. He also had to admit that he had spent the deposit he'd been given and couldn't pay it back.

Prince Nochyn's father was furious and threatened to declare war on Transylvania Waters

---

[49] *Because this book has a Prologue at the beginning, it has to have an Epilogue at the end or else it won't balance properly.*

unless his honour was satisfied.

'I have another daughter,' said the King hopefully.

Howler entered the room, and it was love at first sight – but only from Howler's point of view. Prince Nochyn didn't want to catch a second sight of her, so he jumped out the window and ran away. Howler was about to go and live in a remote cave and give up all hope of love and happiness when something crawled out of number seven cesspit at the sewage works and winked at her. But that is another story.

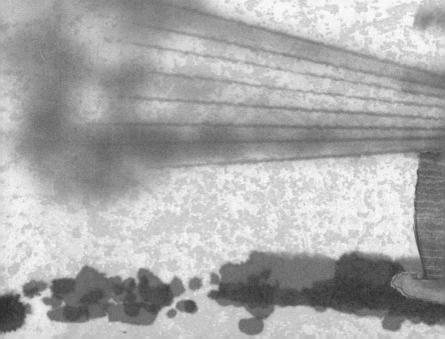

'You will be hearing from our solicitors,' said the King of Battenberg, 'and our very big noisy guns.'

But *that* is another story too.

Another Story

HAPHAZARD HQ QUARTERS
NOT! !
APPROVED BY THE BORING COMICS WITH NO BLOOD AUTHORITY
THE JUNIOR WIZARD'S FUN WEEKLY
SPECIAL
CREEPING SLIME EDITION!
INSIDE - FREE MAP OF THE WHOLE WORLD!
South Pole

North Pole

Belgium

Lake Kevin

Fish

Africa (Probably)

Tuesday

East Pole

The Bermuda Triangle

Australia

The Coffee Ring Islands

Vampire Beetles and other Useful Creatures

How many times have you been out somewhere and thought 'I could just fancy a drop of blood right now', only to find that all the shops are shut and there is no one around who will let you bite their neck?

If you're anything like me, I bet that's happened to you lots of times. You know what it's like, nothing else will do, you just have to have blood. Well, all you need are a few VAMPIRE BEETLES in your pocket and you need never go without the precious sweet sticky red stuff again. Simply place the beetles on your neck, wait a few minutes and then stick their head in your mouth and suck. Sure, it's your own blood you'll be drinking, but what could be better?*

Of course, Vampire Beetles will also clean your teeth like it says in the story, but do be careful not to leave them in your mouth for too long or else they could suck out all your blood, which would make them so fat you wouldn't be able to get them out of your mouth and it would probably make you dead too.

The Ratopedia

Have you ever needed to know about something, but were too lazy to get up and fetch the encyclopedia or search on Google? I know I have. Well, you need the RATOPEDIA. Simply wave a lump of cheese in the air and Ratty will come running. Before you give him the cheese, shout out the word you want to know about and your faithful rodent will flip his back open at the right page.

Magnetic Homing Slugs

If you're one of those people who gets lost really easily, like Winchflat Flood,* Magnetic Homing Slugs are exactly what you need. When you're inside your house you stick them on the fridge, where they absorb bits of food out of the air. When you go out, you put a couple of slugs in your pocket and if you get lost you just put them on the ground and they will head back to their home fridge.

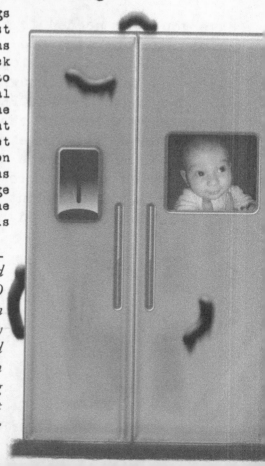

Unfortunately, slugs don't move very fast so it can take months to find your way back home. Also, you have to avoid big electrical stores in case the slugs pick up the scent of mass fridges and get lured away. One person spent three months living inside a huge superstore before he realised it wasn't his home.

---

* Winchflat may be the Flood family genius, but he is SO brilliant there is no room inside his head for ordinary things like being able to find his own front door. When he is working on something really complicated, he can't even remember where the bathroom is, or his left foot.

THE FLOODS 4
SURVIVOR

The youngest child in the Flood family, Betty, is a pretty little girl, who looks quite normal – unlike some of her brothers and sisters. She goes to the normal primary school down the road and she even has a normal best friend, Ffiona Hulbert.

But Betty is not normal – she is a witch. When Bridie McTort, the school bully, starts throwing her weight around, Betty knows exactly what to do. And when Ffiona's dad gets bullied at work, Betty knows how to fix that too.

Meanwhile, Winchflat Flood has been watching old Frankenstein movies and has decided he wants to build a human of his own . . .

OUT NOW!

THE FLOODS 5
PRIME SUSPECT

It was a dark and moonless night and in the blackness something stirred . . .

There's been a murder at Quicklime College and the world's most famous Forensic Special Investigator, Grusom, has been sent to investigate. With the help of his super-smart new assistant, Avid, and a can of magic beans, Grusom unearths the clues that will help him find the murderer. In no time, he has five suspects. Their names are Winchflat, Morbid, Silent, Merlinmary and Satanella Flood . . .

Will the Floods be able to stay hidden from the law – and from the evil enemy who is secretly following their every move – until they can prove their innocence?

OUT NOW!

Promise me that, no matter what happens, no matter how desperate you feel, no matter who asks you, you will never, never, never, read this book.

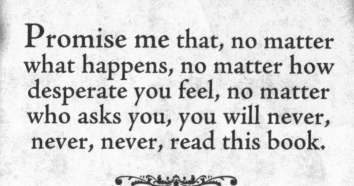

Hidden behind the hundreds of secret doors in the museum, Peter will find an enchanted world, a cursed book and a terrible choice that could change his life for eternity.

HOW TO LIVE
FOREVER

Colin Thompson